by

Alice

Hoffman

Little, Brown and Company

Time Warner Book Group
1271 Avenue of the Americas, New York, NY 10020
Visit our Web site at www.lb-teens.com

First Edition: September 2005

Library of Congress Cataloging-in-Publication Data
Hoffman, Alice.
  The foretelling / by Alice Hoffman. — 1st ed.
     p.   cm.
  Summary: Growing up the daughter of an Amazon queen
who shuns her, Rain rebels against the ways of her tribe
through her sister-like relationship with Io and her feelings
for a boy from a tribe of wanderers.
  ISBN 0-316-01018-9
  [1. Amazons — Fiction. 2. Kings, queens, rulers, etc. —
Fiction. 3. Mothers and daughters — Fiction. 4. Fate and
fatalism — Fiction. 5. Coming of age — Fiction. 6. Sex
role — Fiction. 7. Black Sea Region — Fiction.] I. Title.
PZ7.H67445Fo 2005
[Fic] — dc22   2004025102

10   9   8   7   6   5   4   3   2   1

Printed in the United States of America
Book design by Alyssa Morris
The illustrations for this book were created digitally by Matt Mahurin.
The text was set in Perpetua, and the display type is La Figura.

You are the prophecy.

You are what is to come.

In the
Time

I WAS BORN OUT OF SORROW, so my mother named me Rain.

Ours was a time of blood, when the sky reached on forever, when one horse became a hundred and then a thousand, when we wore our hair in long black braids and rode as warriors. Everything we had was given to us by the goddess, and everything we lost was taken away by her.

We lived in the time of fortune, in a world of

only women. We were warriors from the very beginning, before we were born. There was no battle we could not win. We were strong, the strength of a thousand sisters. And we had something no one else had. Something that caused terror in our enemies when we came across the steppes. Something no one in the man's world had yet managed to do.

We rode horses.

It was said my great-grandmother the Queen had found a white mare in the snow and that she lay down beside this wild creature to warm herself and keep herself alive. My great-grandmother whispered certain words in the mare's ear that no man would ever think of saying. Ours was a country of snow for half the year, of ice and wind and the steppes that led to the Black Sea. By the time the ice had melted, my great-grandmother had made the first bridle out of her leather belt and the snow mare let herself be ridden. A horse and a Queen had become sisters; when they raced across the steppes they were two hearts pounding with a single thought in mind.

Horses were everything to us. Our goddess, our sisters, our sustenance. Alive, they were our way to win battles; four legs against men's two. Even when our horses' lives were gone they were our tents, our clothes, our boots, our food, our traveling companions to the next world. Our children were raised on mares' milk. It made us wild and quick and unafraid. It gave us the ability to speak the language of horses.

A language men had yet to learn.

In the time of our people we lived without men, as we always had. Men were our enemies, a distant, bitter land that came to try to defeat us, again and again. They called us Amazonia. They cursed us and our grandmothers. In their stories they vowed that we were demons, that our skins were blue, that we ate men for breakfast and had bewitched the entire race of horses to become not our sisters but our slaves. They wanted all that we had — our land, our cities, our horses, our lives. They thought women should be worthless, wives and slaves like their own kind.

We were too strong ever to be worthless. We gave in to no one, not the tribes from the eastlands, or the city of stones to the west, not the wild northern men from the ice mountains, not the wanderers who came from everywhere, searching for new kingdoms formed from our age-old land. They all dreamed the same thing: Our land would be named after their foolish kings. Our women would belong to them, walking behind them, in the dust.

But they couldn't defeat us.

They came to destroy us, but in the end they always ran from us in fear, thinking we were fiends — half-woman, half-horse, with the courage of both.

Blood made us stronger, and our fallen came back to us in our dreams and helped us in battle. Our Queen, Alina, was a gift from the goddess, beloved by all, but as unreachable as the stars, especially when it came to me, her own daughter. She was as cold to me as the white stones in the river, as distant as our winter country, far beyond the steppes. Deborah, our high priestess who could see the future and who knew the past, told me what had happened to my mother. Why she was so indifferent; why she'd never asked to see me, just the two of us, mother and daughter, so she could braid my hair, or tell me a story of the world and wars she'd seen.

Her story was not one she wanted to tell.

Some stories are born out of misery and ashes and blood and terror. Tell one of those and your mouth may blister. Your dreams may be turned inside out.

But the priestess whispered my mother's story to me with the voice of a raven, low and raspy with the knowledge of hardship and pain. Our enemy had trapped Alina when she was just a girl. Maybe they could tell she was to be our Queen, as her mother and grandmother had been, as I would be when my time came. Fifty men against a single one of our warriors, a warrior who happened to be a thirteen-year-old girl, my mother, Alina.

They knew how to be cowards. That's what the priestess said. One of them was my father, and Deborah told me that whatever strength all fifty had was now mine. I had stolen it from them, and it rightfully belonged to me along with my yellow eyes. I was stronger than all fifty of those dishonorable men, the enemies who thought my mother would die when they were done with her, who left her on the steppes at the time when the ground was mud and there was the buzzing of flies and the wheat and grass grew tall.

After she was found, my mother was bathed in a cauldron of mares' milk, then given the bark of the laurel tree to chew for the pain of being violated and, more, for the gift of prophecy. Was it any wonder she didn't want to look into the future any more than she wanted to be reminded of the past? My mother wasn't interested in prophecies, or in any future that might be. She spat out the laurel. It was the here and now she claimed for herself. Alina was like a piece of ice in the sunlight, blinding and bright and unforgiving. Our people say the shadow is one of our souls, and my mother's shadow disappeared on the day she was violated. It shattered into black shards, then rose up like smoke. All that was left was the iron inside her; only the hardest part remained.

People told me that when I was born my mother kept her eyes closed; even then she would not cry out, though my birth was said to be difficult, with too much labor and too much blood. Nearly the end of her, it was rumored.

No wonder the Queen was cold. No wonder her hair was so black the ravens were jealous.

No wonder she looked away whenever I passed by.

My own mother whose blood ran through me, whom I was to follow onto a throne of bones and river rocks, never once touched me.

That was how I came to believe I was only sorrow, only rain, and that there was nothing more inside me.

But there was a voice beyond my mother's silence.

I was raised by Deborah and the other priestesses, the sacred prophecy women who wore black robes dyed with hazel. The songs that were my lullabies were Deborah's songs, and each one told me I was fit to be the Queen. My first taste of the world, even before mares' milk, was the taste of the laurel; that's what the old women put in my mouth as soon as I was born, before anything else. Unlike my mother, I swallowed it; I let the laurel grow inside me. The green and bitter taste of prophecy. In time it would be mine.

The priestesses had trained Alina to be our Queen, and now they were training me, the next in line, the girl who would be Queen of a thousand sisters, Queen of a thousand queens. Because Deborah was the oldest and wisest of all, she taught me most of what I knew — how to sew with thread made of horsehair, how to carve spoons out of bones, how to make tea out of the hemp plants and dye clothes with crimson berries and black nutshells. But she also taught me the thing there are no words for.

She believed in me. Not as sorrow. Not as shame.

Deborah took me away so none of the other prophecy women would hear, not even her blood-daughter, Greeya. Deborah had a secret, one to share with me alone. When we were in the place where the wind was so strong it rattled the core of my bones, she whispered that because I was not one but fifty, in time my strength would grow in ways no one could imagine. I would be a warrior like no other. She told me that in spite of my past and my terrible beginnings, I alone could lead our people.

One day I would open my eyes and I would have a vision no one else could see: a sign of what the future might bring.

The warriors closest to my mother, Asteria and Astella, trained me to be their sister-at-arms. Before long I could shoot an arrow nearly as straight and as far as they could. Those two were fearless, with faces painted ochre. They were cousins, but nothing alike, except for their bravery and their silence.

Astella had long black hair plaited into a hundred braids. Asteria had used a dull iron knife to shave the hair from her head; all that her enemies could see when she approached was the blue tattoo on her skull — the image of a bear, the highest mark of courage in battle. Though Asteria and Astella were kind to me, their greatness and their silence frightened me.

Some of the stories told about our people were true. Some cut off their breasts with a hot metal scepter, and they didn't once cry out with pain. But that was only true of those who were archers of the first degree, women like Asteria and Astella who belonged to the goddess completely. The bravest of all.

I felt more comfortable with my mother's sister, Cybelle, the keeper of the bees. She hummed like the bees do; she sang to them with such a sweet voice they followed her through the steppes, past the grasslands, into the houses she made for them.

Bees were the other gift no men had yet been granted, along with horses. Of course, you cannot tame bees the way you can horses; they were not our sisters in that way. But you can live alongside them, Queen to Queen, warrior to warrior. You can learn from their sisterhood: how they follow their Queen no matter what, how battle is nothing to them, how they enter into it freely and fight to the death.

Six women made a vow to follow Cybelle; each one had a sweeter voice than the next and each one smelled like clover. The bee women plaited their hair in a single braid, like Cybelle; they coated their hair with the richest honey, so the bees circled round them, dizzy from the scent. These women knew how to hollow out fallen logs so there would be a place for the bees to make their houses, and how to use smoke to clear out those houses when need be, just long enough to take the honey. Not all of it, of course. There was enough for us all. The bees were our neighbors, good neighbors, better than most. We cared for them, and they for us.

If only it had been that way with all our neighbors.

We were warriors because we had to be; the world we lived in was a battlefield. In truth, everything of importance that I knew about being a leader I learned from my mother, the woman without a shadow. It was not that she instructed me — she who would not speak to me or look at me — but that I studied her from afar. When my mother rose up from the steppes where they'd left her for dead she arose as something new. She had no pity and no regret. She cut through her enemies as though they were wheat and nothing more.

On the wood and leather quiver in which my mother kept her bronze-tipped arrows, there were forty-eight small red half moons, marks for the men she'd killed in battle. They weren't the fifty cowards from the time before my birth, but they would do. As a child I saw her in battle only once, when men from the other side of the Black Sea attacked us while we slept. The children were woken and herded together, but I saw Alina and her warriors run for their horses. I understood then why my mother was our Queen. She was like a whirlwind I could not keep sight of: She rode crouched low on her horse, as though they were one, skin-to-skin sisters.

All the while the Queen raced across the steppe her scythe was directed at the enemy; it was as though in exchange for her lost shadow she had been granted the power to guide her horse not with touch but with a single thought, as my great-grandmother had done. This was the power of a true warrior. Her mind. Her will.

On her hands, my mother wore a pair of lions' claws my grandmother had given her. In battle, she was terrible. A lion with long black hair. Some people said the men she fought were hypnotized by her. They dropped to their knees when they saw her. She appeared to them as a monster who was beautiful beyond belief. How could they fight her? What could they do?

Our enemies ran from her and scattered like leaves, red leaves, fallen leaves.

I thought that was what a true leader was, fierce and victorious, as my grandmother had been and my great-grandmother and now my beautiful and brutal mother. I thought what the world we were living in was, it always would be. I didn't understand that one season was quickly devoured by the next, leaving behind bones and memories. I was watching that happen, the way I watched the clouds move past us, high above our people.

We lived in a time of sorrow and blood, the time of Queens and cruelty, where every man was our enemy, and every horse lost in battle could mean a warrior's life.

Wave after wave of our enemies came. More all the time. They wanted open land like ours. We had so much of it the earth stretched from summer to winter, from the parched yellow lands to the mountains. Time after time we defended ourselves. Blood, heart, bones were strewn across the steppes. There for the birds to pick at. There to sink into the yellow earth. We didn't think whether we were wrong or right to live the way we did, or whether there was another way. We didn't mourn the men whose spirits we took. It was the time of fighting well or dying instead.

When I heard Astella and Asteria's war cries, I shivered. I did not feel like a coward, but I felt different from the women who charged out onto the steppes, their scythes and bows raised, courage their only shield.

One day Astella came back from the battle with her face cleaved nearly in two; the mark of an enemy's axe that would scar her forevermore. She had to be carried to her tent, and watched over through the nights. When she recovered she would no longer walk by the river lest she see herself. She who was afraid of nothing was now reminded of true terror by a single mark of war, a war that never seemed to end, that came to us as surely as the fat white moon.

Even when I was too young to go to war, I understood what it meant: Some of our sisters never returned. At night, their ghosts wandered the steppes, so cold in winter their bones rattled, so parched in summer their shadows burned to ash in the tall yellow grass. Could there be a reason for so much death, one only a Queen or a prophecy woman could understand?

Someday I would be Queen. It was my destiny. But I could not wait for an answer. My head was filled with the fallen. Especially when the rain fell, they seemed to be by my side.

I went to Deborah, the wisest of all. We walked to the windy place that made me feel hollow inside. It was far out in the grasslands, a place that seemed made at the beginning of all things. The goddess was everywhere around us. I felt tiny under the huge sky above us. I could see the shadows of the warriors we had lost in the yellow dust.

I could not yet see the future, but I wanted knowledge poured into me. I wanted my questions answered. I asked why our people had to give their lives in battle. Why the goddess didn't protect us from such a fate. Deborah whispered so that no one else could hear. Her voice sounded like the voice of the raven, difficult to understand, yet perfectly clear.

We are only an instant, that's true. But we are eternal.

In the
Dreams

IN THE DREAMS OF our people there was always a horse.

As infants we rode in the arms of the women who raised us. Our first lullabies were made out of women's voices and of horses, bone and hide and hair. The echo of a thousand hooves on the yellow earth, hot breath that melted the snow, manes that were our blankets, the wind that sang us to sleep as we galloped, flying over rocks and grass-lands and streams.

In every dream I'd ever had there was a black horse, the same one, every time. He was far away, past the grasslands, in the tall mountains we had to cross to reach our winter campground. He was so distant, yet I could see him clearly: storm cloud–colored, onyx-colored.

In dreams I could not catch the black horse, no matter how I might try. Some mornings I woke from sleep, breathless, my legs aching as though I had run all the way to the sea. When I opened my eyes all I could see were the prophecy women, dressed in their dark robes, breathing softly, like horses, sleeping beneath their horsehide blankets.

As the next leader in battle, I needed to learn every skill, from weaving to throwing an axe. To understand is to command, that's what Deborah had told me. That's what she had told my mother when Alina was a girl.

I learned from the best. Asteria taught me to use the axe and the bow, but it was Astella who had taught me to ride. I spent as much of my childhood among the horses as I did with the priestesses, and by the time I was twelve had become the best rider of any girl my age, nearly as good as Astella herself. The other girls distrusted my skill. Even some warriors were jealous: I could stand in a field and wild horses would come to me, unafraid. I could ride for hours and never tire. I spoke our sisters' language, just as Astella had instructed me. I had learned to be one with a horse, not to fight it or force it, but to be a sister through and through.

I thought horse thoughts. I dreamed horse dreams. They were all filled with grass and open sky and the steppes that stretched on forever, wild thoughts and dreams for which there were no words in our own language.

When I rode I was no different from the creature I rode upon. The wind was the same to both of us. The ground shuddered beneath us.

I was ready to ride into battle, but none of our people had her own horse until her thirteenth summer. That was the passage into the life of a warrior: the gift of a horse.

When my time came, I waited for the gift I was sure would come from my mother. I watched the Queen on her great gray mare whose name meant Pearl, just like the precious ring Alina wore on her right hand. But my mother still wouldn't look at me, not even when I brought her mare to her, brushed and shining like the inside of a shell from the farthest shore of the Black Sea.

I waited throughout my thirteenth summer. Astella waited with me, assuring me our Queen would know it was my time. Time to be a warrior and to ride my own mare. But the summer moved forward and there was nothing. Heat waves, hawks, clear white-hot skies. No sign of our Queen.

One evening when I was feeding the horses, Asteria rode up to meet her cousin. Now that Astella's face had been cleaved in two she looked like a reflection in the river, distorted and watery; her left eye was always filled with tears. She looked like a weakling while Asteria, with her shaven skull decorated with its fierce bear tattoo, seemed too ferocious to speak to. I stayed where I was, feeding the horses.

You're not crying over that stupid girl, are you? Asteria said to her cousin. *Little Yellow Eyes.*

It took me a while before I realized she meant me. I was the stupid one. A girl and nothing more. I looked down and saw my feet were coated with dust. I felt I was disappearing. No one could see me.

I'm not crying at all, Astella responded to her cousin. Of the two, she might have been the fiercer in battle, even though her hair was long and her face destroyed. She did not give up easily and her bravery was legend. It was said she pulled the enemy's axe out of her own flesh without once crying out loud.

What's fair is fair, Astella said. *Rain is thirteen and it's time for her to have a horse of her own.*

I'll tell the Queen. Asteria laughed. I was the one who fed and watered Asteria's horse. I was the one to calm her war-horse if a snake or a hawk passed by. *I'm sure it's her main concern.* She smirked. *You can see how our Alina dotes on her daughter.*

I understood. I was nothing to my mother. Sorrow and no more.

And then one day when I rose from sleep with thoughts of the black horse in my head, I heard something outside my tent. Right away I recognized the pure high voice of the one who would be my horse. I ran outside into the already-cold morning. Summer was leaving, but it was not too late. I was still thirteen.

I wished it had been my mother who had chosen my horse. I wished she had been the one to come to me with my gift. But there was Astella holding on to the training rope. She had been working with a wild mare secretly, all summer long.

The horse I was given was white, just as my great-grandmother's horse had been. She was too beautiful to be spoken to, so I called her to me by bowing and lowering my head the way I'd seen the wild horses do. I called my sister-horse our word for Sky, and like the sky, Astella said, she would always be changing. In winter, my mare would disappear in a world of snow, just what a warrior wanted, to be invisible to her enemy. In the summer, the yellow dust would rise up from the steppes and cling to Sky, and once again she would disappear in battle. Our enemy would not see my mare until she was upon them, with me on her back, my slingshot or bow aimed low at the scattering man-beasts.

There were some little children who were afraid of Astella now because of the way she looked, the deep wound that split her face to the bone. But I went to her and dropped to my knees; I swore my gratitude forevermore.

Stand up, Astella said. *I am the one who is grateful. I vow my loyalty.*

For an instant I felt that all things were possible.

That I was, indeed, a Queen.

All through my thirteenth year I practiced. I did not stop until I was the rider I imagined my great-grandmother must have been. I wanted to ride as she had, flying with my eyes closed, better than anyone. It was pride and something more: It was who I was.

In time I could stand on my horse's back and ride at full speed. I could turn around twice, then three times, then four. I could ride hidden from view, backward, so I could spy if there were enemies behind me. Other girls laughed and ran through the grass and swam in the river. As for me, I rode. Even when I was better than anyone else, it wasn't enough. I wanted to ride through clouds. I wanted to ride into dreams. I wanted to go faster than any woman ever had before, and if others envied me for that, so be it.

It was a man who actually helped me do what others could not, who gave me the gift that allowed me to surpass even Astella. He was the single man who lived among us, captured long ago, a smith who'd been made lame so he could not run away. They say that smiths are magicians and the things they make out of iron and bronze and fire are the work of the goddess, her blood and bone. Our man made bronze arrowheads and heavy scythes, the best we'd ever had. For my horse, he fashioned something special.

For the next Queen, he said to me in his broken language. Most of our people stayed away from the smith. He was ugly and his voice sounded like stones hitting together, but he didn't seem like a monster. Perhaps he was hoping for his freedom someday when he spoke kindly to me, waiting for the time when I would be Queen. Perhaps I'd grant it to him in exchange for his gift.

Our stirrups were flimsy, usually made out of horsehide, but the smith made mine of brass covered by hide. These were so strong they could hold my weight as if I were a feather or a single blade of grass. Because of them I could do what other riders could not. I rode with one foot in the stirrup, a part of my white mare, a cloud to her sky. I crouched beside my mare, close to one side. Then I stood and leapt over her back to the other side. I practiced for battle, when I would slip beneath Sky, riding under her belly with her like the sky over me, protecting me.

Covered with snow, I looked like a ghost, fierce as a spirit from beneath the ice. And then when spring came, and the wheat and grass came alive, I turned green with the fresh new world. I knew people spoke of me when they thought I couldn't hear; they called me the *Dream Rider* because I did things others could only dream about. They all gathered round when they heard my horse could leap the water at the bend of the river. But of all the people who came to watch the jump Sky and I had practiced hundreds of times, one was missing.

The only one who mattered to me.

We did not touch the water. We clattered onto the rocks on the other side. A whoop went up from the other side. But I hardly cared.

She never came to see.

When the men from beyond the north came the following summer, the earth was white and yellow, sober and brittle and sharp. There hadn't been much rain and the land had become hard-packed. There was drought, and drought meant war. People wanted water, they wanted our river.

Our priestesses told us that the hard land meant our success in all things. We expected nothing less. The men who came over the steppes

had fought and conquered the red-haired men of
the north storms and now they thought they
would conquer us. They were beasts from the icy
lands. Half-man, half-animal was the word that
preceded them, adept at the axe, wild as wolves.
They believed they'd found the land of a thousand
wives, but instead they had found death. Ours or
theirs, only the battle would reveal.

I dreamed again of the black horse on the night
before war. When I woke everything was silent.
This time I wouldn't be staying home with the
children. I had passed a warrior's rightful age. I
had been given the gift of a horse. Everything I
had ever learned would be put to use in the days
to come.

I would live or not depending on how good a
student I had been.

When our enemies first saw us we must have
looked like bees as much as we did women,
streaked yellow, screaming for war, riding our

horses as though we were flying over the tall grass, over the hardpacked earth. There seemed to be thunder even before we reached our enemy, at least to our own ears. To them we hoped we sounded exactly like what we were: their defeat.

I rode to battle with the prophecy women, the women in black. After the fighting, they took care of the dead. I wanted to ride with the archers, alongside Asteria and Astella, but Astella instructed me to stay with the youngest warriors, whose duty it was to protect our priestesses and then help them send our people on to the next world if they should fall. We buried many in that time. We washed them clean and covered them with honey. We sent them to the next world with their weapons beside them.

The battle was right in front of us. I wanted to get on my horse and ride into the middle of the war. I had to pinch myself to keep from whispering in my horse's ear to ride the way we did when we practiced, faster than the ravens could fly, fastest of all.

We could hear screaming and the cold sound of iron and brass. We could smell blood, a thick scent that filled up your head so that you couldn't see or hear. Our fallen were brutally killed, hacked up, often unrecognizable. I stumbled upon Jarona, an archer not much older than myself. When I saw what they'd done to her, I made a gasping noise and shamed myself by bringing up all that I'd eaten that day, a few bites of meat and some mares' milk.

But we had so many of our dead to collect I stopping thinking about what I was doing and kept to my work. We spoke idly, to forget about blood. I told my dreams of the night before. The only dream I'd ever had was of a black horse. Without warning, a priestess leaned over and slapped me.

Deborah grabbed me away. I didn't fight her. I listened when the high priestess spoke; I was in awe of her great gift of prophecy.

Keep your dreams to yourself, she told me.

Then Deborah whispered what the dream of the black horse meant. It meant death. We had dogs that followed our camp, some of which lived in the tents; it was said these dogs alone could see that same black horse, the earthly form of the Angel of Death, a creature that was invisible to most eyes. Except, it seemed, to mine.

Every dog was howling that day. They saw that the Angel could not be stopped, not by arrows, not by the battles we fought, not by any dreams.

Half of our people were lost in the fields, and those who came back were covered with blood. Our sisters left teeth and bone and flesh in that place where the grass was so tall men could easily hide, at least for a while. Until we were done with them.

When the battle was over the silence reminded me of the silence that followed my dream. Our people were quick to depart from the dead of our enemies, leaving them to the wolves and the ravens. I alone got off my horse to look at the defeated, but I didn't find what I was searching for. A man with yellow eyes, like mine.

By staying behind, I saw things our people

turned away from when they rode away in victory. All around me were the faces of the fallen. They were our enemy, but their agony was a bitter thing to see, especially those who were still in our world, although barely. Blood ran from them and made black pools. I tried not to think of the creatures as human, but as something else, as beasts.

All the same, when I walked through what was left of them, I felt something rising inside me. Our word for this is never used. It is a curse upon our own people when speaking of our enemies.

Mercy.

I chased away all the ravens, running after them until they took flight. Then I shouted the word we must never say aloud in the field of the dying. Before it was spoken, it burned my mouth.

That is why it was forbidden. It hurt too much to say.

After a battle, our people celebrated. We did not lose because we could not. Victory was not a matter of choice; it was a necessity, life itself. Losing meant our people would be gone, a drop of blood on the hard yellow ground. Disappeared.

Our people painted their faces with cinnabar and ochre; they dressed in amulets and amber. They drank koumiss, the fermented mares' milk that made them so dizzy even the wounded could remember how to laugh.

That was how our people rid themselves of the memory of battle: the way men screamed like children, the way our people were cut to pieces when they fell from our sister-horses onto the ground. We forgot in a dreamworld of our own making; we drank and danced until the recent past was far away, and then, farther still.

Sometimes after a war had been won there was a festival that men were brought to, those we had captured and had let live. But a girl could only go if she had killed three men in battle; that meant she was a woman as well as a warrior, ready to have a child. Babies grow into warriors, and that was who we were.

Our Queen never went to the festival. She had no need for men; she already had her daughter. Not that she looked for me after the battle with the men from the ice country. A person didn't need the gift of prophecy to understand how she'd come to name me Rain, to mark the thousands of tears she might have cried the day the fifty cowards trapped her.

All the same, the battle had been my first taste of war. I thought perhaps I might approach the Queen and ask for a blessing. That I might ask for guidance so that in the next battle I would slaughter as many men as came before me, fifty if possible, a hundred if I could, like a true Queen-to-be.

When we returned to our city of tents, my mother went to the edge of the stream where we took our water in summer. I followed her. She was giving gratitude to the goddess. She was the Queen, but humble still.

I was about to go forward when I saw that there was a woman standing in the shadow of the Queen. She was a slave from the north, with

ropes of red hair, long-limbed and fair, forced
into servitude by the enemy we had vanquished.
The slave was covered with tattoos — not the
blue-black lines we wore on our cheekbones and
wrists to mark our blood and our battles. Every
bit of her face and body was covered by red cir-
cles and swirls that could make you dizzy if you
stared for too long, images that moved should
you happen to blink.

When my mother knelt to drink from the
stream, the slave hurried before her and drew the
water for our Queen. She got down on her hands
and knees. I heard my mother say, *You don't have to
do that. You're free here.*

Instead of asking for a blessing, I crouched beside the rocks. I heard the river rushing as though
it was inside my own head. I had never heard such
kindness from the Queen, certainly never for me.

I saw that the swirling things tattooed on the
slave's body were snakes; in some places this was
the mark of a woman forced to give her body
away to men. There were scars down her back
and arms, made carefully, purposefully, to bind
her to her owner. I could see sorrow all over her.

Her name was Penthe — it sounded like a breath when my mother said it.

My mother didn't turn from the slave's sorrow as she turned away from me. I knew love when I saw it, as clearly as I knew sorrow. Penthe took my mother's hands. There was blood and dirt caked on the Queen's hands, but Penthe kissed them both, at the wrist, in the place where we are tattooed for the very first time.

I was jealous to see that my mother could love someone.

Penthe shared the Queen's tent from that first night. If anyone thought it improper for a Queen to lie alongside one who'd been a slave, they didn't dare speak of it.

I didn't realize until the next morning that Penthe had not come to us alone. Sleeping in that crumpled heap by the side of the Queen's tent was Penthe's daughter, Io. I was sneaking up to hear what went on when two women were in love, when I stumbled upon her. A chalky girl with the same long red hair as her mother. The henna tattoos covered half her face and most of her arms. She was my age, but the tattoos were the mark that she'd been used by men. I had already decided to hate Penthe, and I quickly decided to hate Io as well. Meanness rose inside of me. I thought of the blessing I hadn't gotten from my mother.

Don't look at me, I told Io.

She did not truly understand our language. She stared at me and wouldn't stop.

Our people had been taught not to get too close to the Queen, out of respect, certainly, but also out of fear. Because I was to be next, people knew to avoid me as well. The girls my age especially had little to do with me, more so since I had become the best rider of all. They got out of my way and that was fine with me. I did as I pleased, alone, the way I liked it. Always alone.

But Io knew none of this; she followed me from the beginning. She called me *sister,* though I ignored her. She was afraid of things and I laughed at her. Why shouldn't I? She was nothing to me. A wisp. A frightened slave. She cared nothing about being a warrior. She was especially afraid of horses. While we were training, Io sat sewing with thread made from a horse's tail, fixing a tear in my tent. When she saw Cybelle's beehives she was so terrified by the buzzing within, she hid behind a tree. I must have wanted her to be afraid; that day I helped Cybelle smoke the bees away and I fanned the smoke in Io's direction.

When the bees chased her, Io screamed and ran and I laughed. I had no need of a sister or anything else.

I've never seen you so mean, Cybelle said. *Will you be a cruel Queen when your time comes?*

We were coated in mud to make sure that the bees, our good neighbors, wouldn't sting us. It was wise to be careful even with the best of friends.

Isn't every Queen cruel? I asked. *Even among bees? As for Io, let her run. All the way back to the north storm country where she belongs.*

The weak are cruel, Cybelle said to me. *The strong have no need to be.*

However mean I might be, Io insisted on following me. Cruelty didn't seem to matter in this case. She remained convinced she belonged to me; even when I rode my horse as fast as I could, she ran after me, trudging along until she was covered with yellow dust with bits of grass threaded into her red hair.

Worst of all, Io had taken to sleeping outside my tent. Penthe had told her she must find a place for herself, and none of the other girls would have anything to do with her. People were laughing at her curled up with a blanket in the chilly night air, and soon they were laughing at me. They said I had a red-haired slave like my mother. She was a know-nothing. Useless.

Go away, I cried. *Leave me be.*

A Queen should not be laughable. Even a Queen-to-be.

But Io wouldn't stop acting as though she were my sister. The crueler I was, the kinder she became. Nothing could get rid of her, not insults, not the red ants I dropped in her blankets that made her itch at night. She continued to sing a beautiful song whose words I couldn't understand.

When I treated her badly, Io didn't seem to notice. Every night she slept beside my tent, shivering, when inside I had extra blankets I didn't care to share. I couldn't stand it anymore; the song she sang in a language I didn't understand got into my dreams. At night, my head was filled with that melody and the black horse that visited me while I slept.

I went outside into the starlight. The whole world seemed dark, except for Io's bright hair. She turned her face to me, happy to see me.

What do you want from me? I said.

Io took off an amulet hung around her neck. It was a strand of leather decorated with seashells from far away, from the land of the north storm country. One shell was white, one was pink, one was the color of the blue ice in the deepest center of winter. Io had me hold the white shell to my ear, and although it was tiny I could hear water.

That's where I come from, she told me.

Why would you give me a gift?

Since our mothers are together that means I'm your sister, Io said.

I would never have a sister like you. Afraid of a shadow.

The things I'm afraid of aren't shadows, Io said.

She sounded different then. When I looked at her I realized she knew more about some things than I did.

When someone owns you they can do whatever they want with you, she told me. *They can burn you, they can tie you with ropes, they can touch you however they want. Whenever. More of them. Anyone they say. You have no choice. You belong to them.*

She said all this blankly, as though these terrible things had happened to someone else. She ran her hands over her arms, where men had tattooed her with red snakes. Then Io told me all about her life before she came to live with us. About the way she had belonged to men who paid for her, and what they'd done to her, and how she'd bit her tongue so hard to be quiet she had bitten right through in one place; that place still hurt her every time she took a drink of water. It was as though a spirit had gotten hold of her and she had fought it off with the spirit inside herself.

The more she spoke, the more I saw something in her that was strong, stronger than those snakes; her will made her tattoos disappear. I didn't even notice them as she spoke. I saw the girl she truly was as though I were looking right through her.

Now I choose, she said. *And I choose you to be my sister.*

After that, I stopped being so mean. I got so used to her that soon whenever Io didn't follow me, the oddest thing happened: I felt alone, and I didn't like the feeling. It made no sense to me.

Every warrior is alone in this world.

Every one must fight her own battle.

In the
Winter

of

THE MOST ALONE TIME FOR OUR PEOPLE was
during the journey we each were commanded to
take at the time of our first blood. It was not so
much a test for bravery, but a search for a vision
of the future. Who would we be in the world of
daylight? Who would we be in our dreams?

It happened to me in my fifteenth winter, in the
season when we moved our city of tents across
the steppes, into caves, when the snow was high.

It was the time when the great bear shone in the sky like a torch. I awoke and found blood on my blanket and my leg. My time had come. Before I left to find my vision, my mother called me to her.

I had been waiting for this my whole life.

Now she would see I was more than sorrow.

I stood before her, eyes down. She was the most beautiful woman in any land. People spoke of her in faraway places, on the other side of the sea, even in the north storm country.

Look at me, she said.

I did so.

The Queen slapped me hard across my face. Something in my ears started to ring. All mothers slapped their daughters on the day of their first bleeding; they did so to welcome them into the world of womanhood, which brought its own pain for which we must be ready.

Every girl was slapped, true enough, but not like this. My jaw was burning but I kept on staring at my mother. Of course she wanted me to be strong. She wanted to see if I could be stronger than fifty men.

But when I looked up at her I could see something more. Something that frightened me. She wanted to hurt me.

Thank you, I said, as though my face weren't throbbing. As though she'd given me a gift and hadn't done what she intended. Caused me pain.

My mother slapped me once more, and this time I tasted blood.

Penthe was there and she took my mother's hand. This woman who had been a slave was bold enough to stop the Queen.

My mother thought better of hitting me again.

I hope your vision comes to you, she said to me.

I know it will. I intend to go and find it.

It had been impossible to hate Penthe as I'd wished to do; she was too beautiful and too good-hearted. Now when she and my mother walked past me, Penthe smiled, then she noticed my mother looked straight ahead, as a Queen should when confronted with sorrow. Penthe followed Alina. She was happy here with my mother, they walked with their arms around each other, they danced together and slept together; they shared everything, even their nightdreams.

The old women said Penthe had come from so far north the snow was as tall as the top of a tree; they vowed that five hundred men had used her for their pleasure, that each of the tattoos that covered her body was to document some man's desire.

Still, she had not forgotten how to be kind. Now as she walked away with the Queen, Penthe turned back to me. She smiled with her eyes.

When I was packing for my journey I saw a shadow outside my tent. It was the smith. I should have ignored him, but I thought about the way he'd been made lame so he couldn't run away. I thought about the fact that none of us spoke his native language; our words probably sounded like stones to him.

When I went out I saw the smith was there because he'd made something for me. Something special. Fit for a Queen-to-be. It was a bronze scythe into which he'd fashioned bees and bears. It was a deadly and beautiful thing. Perhaps what they said about smiths was true, that they were magic-makers. Some people thought such men could show you the future, just as our priestesses did. When they forged metal what was soon to be could be seen in the fire.

How will my journey go? I asked. *Did you see what would happen in the fire?*

You'll need the scythe, was all he said.

Before I left, I was brought to the priestesses and given koumiss to drink for the first time. It was sour at first, then sweet. Because of the power of the koumiss there was no pain when they gave me my first tattoo. They heated the bronze needle over the fire until the iron was red, then blue. They used the dye from the plants that grow along the river.

This is instead of tears, Deborah said to me. *This replaces sorrow.*

One line of darkest blue on my wrist.

One line that burned through the night as I went into the snow.

At night, the center of the universe is above us and the great she-bear is in the sky. The bear is the part of the goddess that rules the blood and the seasons. When the she-bear's tail is to the east it is summer and the grain is green and the earth is yellow and we have all we want to eat. When her tail is to the west it is autumn and we move on to higher ground where there is still food. Our people follow the bear; we never stay in one place for long. We have heard of cities made of stones and bricks, but our city of tents moves, like the stars above us.

When the bear's tail is to the north, as it was on the night of my alone journey, that is when the snow reaches halfway up the horses' legs, when breath turns to crystal and we wear all of our clothes at one time, the leggings made of horse-hide, the shirts of deerskin, the hats of fox and rabbit. Alone of all creatures, the she-bear is un-afraid of winter. She simply disappears into the very depth of it. That is the center of the year, when it is dark nearly all of the time and what lit-tle light that does come is blue.

Because it was my time, my journey, I knew I must think of the bear, and sing to her, and ask her for guidance.

On my night journey I was soon proud of myself. I had tracked a deer in the snow and cut it down with a single arrow. I said a prayer for the gift of the deer, and let out its blood as a gift to the goddess. I had the deer carcass draped over my horse's shoulders and was riding to find a place to make my camp when I saw a shadow. I thought perhaps it was the shadow that my mother had lost when she was violated. Or the shadow of the deer's spirit. I thought I might have made a wrong turn in the snow and crossed into the next world, where we were not supposed to enter until our lives were through.

It was the time of people, but it was also the time of spirits, and I was prepared to meet up with not only those who were in this world, but those who inhabited the next.

I felt a shiver inside me. I stopped and got to my feet. The snow reached over my knees. I was glad I had the scythe with me. It had never been used in battle. At least not yet.

If you're here to kill me, I'll kill you first, I said in a whisper, only loud enough for a spirit to hear.

The snow was still falling and the sky was as white as my horse; even my black hair became white, as though I were already the old woman I might someday be if I didn't die in battle. I hadn't dreamed of the black horse the night before, so I felt secure that death wouldn't come for me now.

Because my boots were made of horsehide I made no sound on the snow, but my breath billowed out. My blood was pounding. There was the shadow before me. Perhaps it was only a dream, but no. It made a noise. It was a ghost noise, a sorry sound, hungry and alone. Motherless. I knew that noise. When I was younger, it had belonged to me, too.

I crouched down and saw that the shadow was a bear cub, somehow forgotten in the center of winter, trapped in a deep snowdrift. I felt something in my heart I hadn't felt before.

I used the scythe to free the cub from the ice-packed drift; when I was done she was too weak to scramble away. I went back to my horse and

fetched a deerhorn filled with mares' milk. I tried to approach but the bear backed away.

It's just me, sister. I moved in and let her lap the milk out of the palm of my hand. I could feel the bear's heat, how alive she was. She drank all the milk.

Now the horse is your mother, I said.

It must have been true, because when I carried the bear to my horse, and tied her into my rolled-up blanket, the mare didn't flinch. Most horses shy from bears, but Sky was fearless. A Queen's horse.

When I returned everyone came to see what I had brought back from my journey, even the Queen. Now they could all see: I had the strength of fifty men. I held a bear across my knees, not dead — any man could have done that — but alive, a sister to me.

I felt my mother's eyes on me. For the first time I think she was seeing something other than sorrow. Maybe she did have the gift of prophecy in some things. Maybe she saw I was the Queen-to-be.

I called the bear Usha, which sounded like our word for the northernmost star. At night, she was kept near the horses, chained up; she would let us know if any creature, man or otherwise, tried to steal what belonged to us. Usha kept watch, like the great bear in the sky. During the day, she was beside me, following as though she wanted to run as fast as Sky did. Usha became like the foal my mare had never had, motherless no more. Perhaps she thought she was a horse; perhaps she dreamt she was. I dreamt sometimes of riding her into battle, terrifying every enemy, a hundred bands of blue on my face. When I was Queen, that's what I would do. People as far as the north storm country and beyond would fear me as they feared Usha; they would stay away and speak of me in whispers. The Queen who was half-horse and half-bear, who might not be human at all, except in her own dreams.

My name may have meant sorrow, but as I neared my sixteenth summer I felt happy. I was afraid to say it aloud because things you say aloud disappear; so I kept quiet, but it was there. My happiness. It was warm again and we had traveled back to the pasturelands. Io and I had lots of time to wander. We took Usha into woods that were so green you had to squint to see. We'd discovered that the bear could lead us to beehives; then we'd run back and tell Cybelle and she'd come with her smoke jars and old hollow logs and talk the bees into giving us their honey, and even coming home with us.

Io kept her red hair braided like ours and she wore the boots that we all wore, horsehide, tied up high with leather strips. But she wasn't like us If you looked into her pale eyes you could see what had happened to her. It was like looking down a well. She spoke of things while she slept, and I was glad she mostly spoke in a language I couldn't understand. *Stay away from me,* she would murmur. I understood that.

Maybe that was why I could be myself with

her, not the Queen-to-be, not the keeper of sorrow. Just Rain. Maybe that was why I took her along with me into the forest, and why I wasn't jealous that Usha seemed to be her sister as well. The bear napped curled up, her head on Io's knee.

I'm afraid to move, Io would say, and we would laugh so hard that Usha would wake up and shake herself.

Watch this, I said one day in the woods.

I'd made a bit, which the bear was now used to, since I'd sweetened the leather with mares' milk. I used a bridle formed of horsehair rope.

I got on Usha's back and whispered for the bear to run. It was so different from horseback, so high, so clear, as though I were a part of the forest, a tree, a green thing, a wild beast. I had to kick to get Usha to stop, and when she wouldn't I leapt off, crashing into ferns and tall grass.

The bear ambled back and licked my face. Her breath was terrible, but it was warm, alive.

Good horse, I told her.

I confided my dream of the future to Io: When I was Queen I would ride a bear into battle. I would be terrible to behold and men would run from me, like fallen leaves, red leaves, scattered before me.

I should have known then that one thing should never pretend to be what it is not. Woman or horse or bear. Being anything other than what you truly are can only lead to sorrow and regret. I should have let Usha be a bear.

That day, Io applauded my bear riding. My little sister, she thought everything I did was wonderful.

We went back through the tall grass. We didn't talk about where I had come from or where she had come from. But I knew she had been right that first day. We were sisters. We had both come from the place of sorrow, and that bound us together, moreso than blood.

One day I went to the smith. I asked him to make a special bridle and stirrups for Io, so that she would not be afraid of horses. And I wanted a scythe for her that was just like mine.

I will make them, he said, *but Io's not like you. She'll never ride. She'll never see battle.*

If you can see her future, what of mine?

You're the one who can see it, the smith said.

The smith picked up sand and threw it into the fire. The dust burned blue.

That was nothing, I said.

Watch more carefully, the smith told me.

Again he reached for a handful of our yellow earth. Again, it turned blue in the fire. And then I saw it. I was riding east, all by myself, into a snowstorm. Behind me were warriors. I outdistanced them, but when I turned I saw there were women behind me, weapons raised. My people.

You know nothing, I said. *Make Io the bridle. And make sure the scythe is as beautiful as mine.*

I walked away. Still, I couldn't stop thinking of the fire-image. There was a world out there I knew nothing of. When I tried to question Penthe about the lands she'd seen, she only said, *Be glad you're here with your mother the Queen.*

I brought my sister Io the bridle when the smith was done, and she wept. *It's too good for me,* she said.

You're the sister of the Queen-to-be, I told her.

I went to my mother and knelt before her, asking her to give Io a horse, and she did. I was frightened to do this. I thought she might turn away, but the Queen heard me out. She looked at Penthe before she said yes, then smiled. I think the gift was more for Penthe's sake than for me or for Io, but that didn't matter. The mare was a roan, red like Io's hair. My sister loved the horse. She combed it and sang to it. She used its hair for her thread so that everything she sewed was red.

But she didn't want to ride. About that, the smith seemed to be right. And she kept the scythe that had been decorated with bees and bears, identical to mine, in a felt blanket as though it were an amulet rather than a weapon.

It was at this time that I became afraid of my dreams. The darkening color of the sky, the stars above, both had become my enemy. I was exhausted, but afraid of the night. I had been dreaming of the black horse again, the Angel of

Death. I had been thinking of the vision I'd seen in the smith's fire.

I went to see Deborah when I stopped sleeping. She took me into the woods, to the place where prophecy could be found, if you knew what you were looking for. It was the place where the wind came to rattle your bones. We both drank the mixture the priestess made of mares' milk and other things. Things no one should drink if they don't want to know the truth.

Deborah threw the augury, the stones and bones she used to read fortunes. She sat back on her heels with a look I hadn't seen on her face before.

I see your enemies, she said.

Do any of them have yellow eyes?

I thought perhaps I might have to fight the people of the fifty cowards. For that fortune, I would be grateful.

They are familiar. Look for yourself.

It was a blur to me. I bent close to see.

They're following you on horseback, Deborah said.

No men did that.

There was a blue line in the center of the augury, the symbol for our people.

My own people turned against me. It was the same fortune I had seen in the smith's fire.

Deborah was so old that the ravens came to sit with her in the evenings to ask her questions. The line between this world and the next was so thin, she could see right through it. She carried her wisdom close to her, but I was brave enough to ask for a tiny bit.

Is there any way to change your fortune? I asked.

I've heard of it.

Well, if it can be done, I'll manage it, I told her. To sound brave was to be brave sometimes. *You'll see it with your own eyes.*

She was a priestess. I should have kept my head bowed when I addressed her, but I did not.

Deborah laughed at my nerve. *I hope I live till then, child,* she said to me. *I hope that you do, too.*

In the
Country

IN THE COUNTRY OF THE QUEEN we did not disobey. We did not even think of it. Except for me. Inside, I had a kernel of something that was made out of fire. Maybe that was where my yellow eyes came from. Maybe I hadn't inherited them from any man; maybe they were from the center of my own being.

I did as I pleased, ignoring my chores. I should have been caring for the horses with Astella, but I did not. I should have been watching over the bees with Cybelle, but I avoided that work as well.

I was spending all of my time riding again. I was the Dream Rider, true enough, and although Sky needed no further training, it was my sister the bear I taught to act like a horse.

If any man had seen me as we practiced, he would have thought I was a demon.

As I might have been.

I was wild, I admit that. I drank mares' milk and so I believed myself to be part horse. I thought myself to be half-bear as well now, invincible, more ferocious than the warriors who as girls made the decision to sear off one breast, ensuring that when they pulled the bow back it would rest flat against their hearts. They were coated with the paste of red flowers, in a trance when the hot iron was placed against them, in a half-trance for days afterward.

I did not have to make that decision; I was the Queen-to-be and must be good at all things, not only warfare. I knew my place was on the throne of bones we carried back and forth across the steppes.

But now, something had changed.

I didn't trust my people the way I had before my future had been told. As the Queen-to-be, I should have had everything, but my hands seemed empty. I'd never been close to the other girls my age; now I moved away even from Io. When she tried to follow me, I told her I needed time and solitude in order to train Usha. Io left me in the woods with my bear. But I could tell, she didn't believe me.

She could sense the doubt I had about my place in our world even if I didn't speak such things aloud.

One day my mother's sister Cybelle came to see me. She wore golden bracelets along her arms. Bees followed her; they buzzed around her hair, which had been plaited with honey. The bear, which had grown more fierce in the woods and less accustomed to people, made a happy noise to greet Cybelle the way she did when I brought her supper. My aunt was that sweet, smelling of clover and honey.

Cybelle told me that people had begun to talk about me. Why was I by myself so much? Why did I not give more service to the Queen?

What does it matter? The Queen doesn't like to look at me.

The Queen looks into the future, at the next war, Cybelle told me. *A Queen needs to lead; that's what is expected of her. Above all else, above her own life and whomever she loves. A Queen has no time for love.*

Cybelle was the sort of person who seemed soft, and then the next moment she was hard and fierce. There was nothing that frightened her. She had been stung a thousand times by our neighbors the bees, and had never once cried out. It was her duty to have the dying brought to her after a battle, those who would be better off in the next world than in this one, and to send them on their journey. She had a gold dagger she used at such times; she never once flinched.

Do you think you will ever be ready to lead us? Cybelle asked me. *Do you think you're able?*

Do you question that? I felt hot with anger. I'd

thought Cybelle valued me as something more than sorrow.

You're the one who questions it, my aunt said.

After Cybelle had left I wondered if my mother had sent her. If the words Cybelle had said had been formed in another's mouth. A Queen who didn't trust me to follow or to lead.

Although I had always assumed I was the Queen-to-be, I wasn't so sure others were in agreement. I needed to test myself, make myself stronger. I needed to follow the path of the bear. To stand and fight for what I wanted. But what was that? Maybe because of the fifty cowards I had fifty thoughts in my head. I who was supposed to lead dreamed of the black horse and heard our enemies' death cries in my sleep.

I didn't know what I wanted, but even then I knew one truth that couldn't be undone. A Queen has but one thought: *These are my people.*

All through my sixteenth summer I searched for a way to change my fortune, to be a leader, to follow my Queen, to stop doubting myself, to wake up from my dreams. I went past the pasturelands and into the forests in the hopes that the goddess would guide me. Wherever I went, Usha followed. My sister the bear was slower than my sister-horse, so we were slow with her. The ride became a dreamy thing, and that is never good.

Dreams should stay where they belong, inside the spirit, inside the night.

But that's not what happened. One day it was green and I was happy just to be with my horse and my bear. I was foolish enough to do what a warrior must never do. I closed my eyes.

They were upon me the way vultures are upon the dying, the dreaming, the already dead. Four red-haired men who all seemed like one to me. One swarm, one demon, one thing tattooed with red henna, the owner of dozens of arrows and too many axes to count. I could hear someone screaming, and it was me. For the first time I truly understood fear — it was like bees under my skin, stinging, stinging. The enemy fell on me and dragged me from my horse, which was invisible in winter and in spring, but not now. Now my horse was as easy to see as the endless sky.

They grabbed me so hard I heard something break. My heart. My soul. I thought of my mother with the fifty cowards, one of them my father, then blinked that thought away. I was not just anyone. I reached for my scythe and killed one quickly, then another was on top of me; I could feel the heat from him. He started to say something in his language, which sounded like the grunting of wild dogs. He must have thought I was listening to him. He gave me just enough time to reach for my scythe, that beautiful harsh weapon, which I brought down so hard I could hear him shatter inside.

I knew these men could not have gotten past Usha; she would have fought to her death. As she did and was now doing. She stood on her hind legs, her mouth open, showing her huge teeth, fighting for me and for herself. But I'd made a mistake. I'd let Usha believe she was a horse; she had no idea of her own strength. She'd never fought like a bear before.

I could see two men upon Usha with axes until the world looked red. I went after them screaming, the scream like bees in my mouth. One of them grabbed me by the throat. His fingers were hot, burning.

From the corner of my eye, I saw someone else. A boy with dark hair like mine. He came round quietly, like a dream, picked up an axe from one of the fallen, and split open the head of the man who was tearing my clothes from me.

The last red-haired man, the one who'd finished off Usha, we chased down together. Through the tall grass. We didn't speak but we planned it. We looked at each other, nodded, understood each other completely. The boy went to the right, I went to the left, the side of the goddess, the she-bear, the bee.

The old women have said it should never give pleasure to kill an enemy, so I will not tell the truth. I will never say how the war cry sounded in my mouth; it was a joyful thing, such sweetness I nearly choked from the taste.

I whistled to call my mare and she came across the grass. Sky was nervous and danced a bit, but she was used to the scent of blood. She let me grab the bridle and take the blanket from her back to wrap around myself. My shirt had been torn away, and I should have been shivering. I should have felt shame. I felt neither of those things. Only victory.

I didn't understand all that the boy said, but enough to determine that the red-haired men were from the north storm country. They had been murdering anyone they met on the steppes, including some from among the boy's people. This boy was taller than me, but the same age. He followed when I walked back to where Usha was. Then I did a terrible thing. I should have cut out my sister-bear's heart to eat so I could honor her. Instead I did what a warrior should never do: I dropped to my knees and wept.

Something was over. Not just the bear's life. Something in mine.

The boy stood there, still, watching me. He

had no weapons of his own, only an axe that had belonged to one of the red-haired men. This axe he threw away, as though it were unclean. He did not seem to mind that he was defenseless before me. I could have killed that boy. But I had no wish to do so. This boy's people were a tribe of wanderers who had lost their way long ago and who now traveled endlessly; he had been everywhere and knew bits of most languages. Now he started to sing one of his people's songs. It was a song to Usha's spirit, I understood that much.

I thanked him in the way I could. I gave him my scythe, the one with the bears and the bees engraved. The one the smith had made especially for me. At first, he would not take it, but I insisted. I grabbed his hands and then he stopped waving the scythe away.

He was my enemy as well, I was sure of it. And yet it didn't feel that way.

When I asked his name he said Melek. He didn't have to tell me more. I knew that in his world and among his people, it meant king.

By the time I rode back to our city of tents, I felt I would never cry again. That girl was gone, and I had returned in her place. Covered with blood, my throat turned blue and yellow with bruises from the grasp of the red-haired man, a scar down my back, still bloody, throbbing with pain. I had killed four men. They were nothing. Flies. Buzzards. Beasts.

But they were the thing that made me what I now was. The daughter of the Queen.

The whisper of my return went before me, and by the time I reached my tent my mother was there. She had some of the priestesses bring me water in the ritual buckets that were made of horsehide. She watched as I took off my blanket and poured water over myself to wash the blood away. I could feel my mother's eyes on me; she seemed surprised that I was a woman, as tall as she.

Did they hurt you? Did they do what they wanted with you?

She wanted to know if the priestesses should

bring me the bark of the laurel tree, the offering for those who'd been violated. I shook my head.

I had fought the wind and lost Usha. I said, *They got nothing.*

Io embraced me and took me back to my tent. She brought me milk and stew. I fell asleep as though I had never been to that country before, but I didn't dream. When I awoke, I saw the scythe that the smith had made for Io had been placed across my blanket.

To replace the one you lost, Io said to me. *Now I'm your sister the bear.*

I could have cried if I'd had any tears.

With you as my sister, Io, I'll never need another, I told her.

Afterward people said that my horse had a fleck of blood between her eyes that wouldn't wash away. They were afraid of her; they whispered that she was marked with death. I think they were also afraid of me. I had defeated men who had killed a bear; in doing so, I had become the bear. I carried Usha with me. I was more silent, and I practiced more with Asteria and the warriors she trained. I was dutiful now, ready to become the Queen. And yet I was still thinking of other things, things I should have closed myself to.

One day when the summer was still hot but slipping away, I rode back to the place where Usha had been killed. My mare almost bolted when we reached the grasslands, but I made her go on. I rode fast and hard; I didn't think of what I was doing. When I stopped, my horse stood on her hind legs and pawed at the air. I whispered to her that this was another time even if it was the same place; when I jumped off I tied her to a low shrub so she wouldn't run away.

I knew I was in the right spot because the ground was red. Nothing grew in this place, not grass, not wheat, not brambles. There were bones outside the circle, picked clean by birds and wild dogs. White as snow.

I looked down to make sure I still had my shadow. There it was, as tall as a tree.

Inside my shadow was a basket, made of reeds.

I knelt down. I could smell Usha here, her blood
in the yellow dirt. I lifted the cover of the basket.

It was a gift for me.

Melek had made Usha's claws into gloves
for me to wear in battle, just as my great-
grandmother had worn the claws of a lion, which
were then given to my grandmother, and then to
Alina, our Queen. It was some time before I
found the courage to reach inside the basket. I
took my sister's paws and slipped them over my
hands. All at once, I felt stronger. I stood and
lifted my arms in the air. I screamed my war cry,
and I let it echo in my head and shake the grass
around me and raise earth into clouds of dust.

What happens when someone gives you a gift? I
felt something inside me that I didn't understand.
I replaced the claws into the basket, which I tied
to my horse blanket. I got back on my horse and
went west. I was not a great tracker, but good
enough to find his people, the wanderers who
had been lost for so long.

It was a small tent village, nothing like our city. But because these people were smiths what little they had shone with light. There were doors made of wood on their tents with brass markings. Their well was made of stones that were pink, carried from some far-off land, perhaps so they would always be reminded of home.

I lay down in the grass and watched his people light their fires, cook their evening meal. Men and women lived together here, and I wished I could see the way they looked at each other, but I was too far away to see their faces. Doves were flushed out of the grass and the beating sound of their wings made me dizzy. I heard something that made my heart race. Some man was playing an instrument I hadn't heard before. It sounded as if his spirit was in the music, rising far above us.

Melek may have been a magician as well. Without being told, he knew I was there. I supposed I was calling to him in some way, and he heard me.

He left his people and came to where I was. He

put his hand up and I did as well; somehow our palms came together. He saw the basket I had tied to my mare. He saw the look on my face before I even knew it was there.

We lay down together in the grass, even though he must assuredly be my enemy. We whispered about the demons we had fought together and the way the earth was still red in our meeting place. We didn't really have to speak. We taught each other some words, but they seemed foolish. Melek ran his finger over the line of blue on my wrist.

There was no need for me to cry.

If this was his kingdom, it wasn't much. No horses, no beehives, no thousand warriors all loyal to a single Queen. But as I lay there, listening to the music for so long I had to spend the night, falling asleep beside him in the tall grass, I thought perhaps he had enough. I wasn't the sort of person who said good-bye. I left while it was dark, walking my horse until we were far enough away for me to slip onto her back and ride away.

I left him my horse blanket, made of red horse-hair thread that Io had braided.

Now he had two things that were precious to me, this King of Nothing. And I had my sister the bear to wear into battle. A fine trade if you asked me.

So why was it I felt I had taken too much? Why did I feel as though I had given too much away?

Somehow Io sensed a difference in me. She was gentle and she didn't ask questions, but she knew me. I had changed. The wild girl I had once been had been replaced by a woman who wasn't certain of anything, least of all the future. At night, Io stayed in my tent; she knew I still couldn't sleep. She thought I had bad memories of Usha's death. She still believed I was the brave one, fearless in battle. But the truth was, I was too afraid to dream. Afraid of the future that had been foretold.

I went to see Deborah. She was so old she had to be carried to the fire by two of the younger priestesses. I had come to get my second tattoo, another line of blue marking the battle I'd fought for Usha. Because I had not been alone in that battle, I felt like a liar, undeserving of any honor.

I brought Deborah a headdress made of raven feathers I'd found in the grass, sewn together with black horsehair thread.

Sometimes a gift is meaningless, sometimes it means the world, Deborah said.

I was frightened by how powerful she was, how she had the ability to know a person from the outside in.

After we'd drunk the koumiss, after they'd burned the blue into my face, I begged Deborah to read my fortune one more time. She sent everyone else away. Her daughter, Greeya, begged to stay. She worried that Deborah was too frail to read the future, but Deborah insisted even Greeya must leave us.

She waited until we were alone. She nodded like the ravens do. Her fingers trembled as she shook the augury box. Inside were beads, shells, bones, two green stones.

I hear rain inside, Deborah said. *Listen.*

The augury box did sound like rain, but then my head was spinning from all I'd had to drink. My face was burning. My tongue was burning, too. Who was I? That's what I wanted to know.

The Queen-to-be or the girl in the grass? Who was I now and who would I soon be?

Deborah threw the augury. Two stones hit against each other and Deborah breathed in as though she'd been hurt.

It's the same, isn't it? I said. *A bad fortune.*

To have any fortune at all is a good thing, Deborah reminded me. *Are you still dreaming of the black horse?*

I don't dream.

I leaned forward when Deborah threw a handful of earth into the fire even though I was afraid to see what might appear. It was the end of summer and the nights were cooler. We could feel the coming winter, the way we could feel the passage of our own lives. Inevitable. Eternal.

Look, the priestess said to me.

There in the fire was the black horse.

And it was I, no one else, who was running beside it.

It was the time of year when the great bear in the sky's tail was moving to the west. Every night, colder. Soon we'd leave the pastureland for high ground where there would be more to eat and we could spend the winter in caves. I didn't want to leave this place. I didn't want the stars to move. The truth of it was, I didn't want anything to change. But none of that was in my hands.

Only my own fortune was there.

In the
Heart

IN THE HEART OF A WARRIOR QUEEN there can be no confusion. She must at all times know who she is and what is expected of her.

She is the fearless, the brave, the murderous if need be.

When my mother's scouts told her that men from the east were moving toward our city, my mother prepared herself for battle. Sometimes the battle comes to you, but there are other times when you must go to battle before it can arrive at your door and destroy you where you live.

This time I would not ride with the prophecy women, but with the warriors. It was what I had always wanted, and yet I felt myself shiver, as though it was already winter. I felt something in my heart, a heaviness, a stone.

We rode for a single day, that's how close these people had come to us. We arrived before the sun came up, so many of us that the dust that arose behind our horses could be seen all the way from our city, or so the old women who'd been left behind later said. Perhaps the men from the east had heard of us and wanted wives; perhaps they'd only blundered into our land. It didn't matter what they intended or what they wanted. Our people wanted things, too.

Firstly, we wanted not to lose our own people. We were warriors, but there were many ways to fight a battle. We knew tactics men had not yet learned or even imagined. Our people waited on the steppe while Cybelle and her beekeeping women went forward in the dark. They smelled so sweet as they entered the village, no one from the eastern people awoke from their dreams. The enemy slept heavily, lulled by a buzzing sound. Carefully, Cybelle and her women used wooden funnels to let the bees enter beneath the tent flaps. No one noticed the bees at first; they slept on long enough for Cybelle and the women to come back to us, like shadows over the rocks, across the steppe, the log bee houses they carried now empty.

All at once, our enemies ran from their tents, shouting, confused, stung by our good neighbors. They had panicked, as warriors never should. The instant they did, we went forward. I could hear my mother's war cry, and I rode along with the women my age, Io's scythe at my knee. I was wearing the bear claws, pulled up to my elbows, so that my wrists were protected by Usha's claws and my hands were free.

Even my own people looked at me differently in this battle, as though I were a sister to the bear. I aimed my arrows and felled two of the enemy. I saw the way they went down into the dust out of the corner of my eye, yet I kept on seeing it. An arm lifted into the air, a thud on the earth, a cry that rose and then disappeared like snow in a fire.

But I was not proud of what I'd done. Usha's spirit must have entered me, and only I knew she was not a warrior, not truly a bear at all, but a horse. I hated what I saw before me and I felt sickened. I could not abide the hot scent of blood. In the midst of battle, I felt as though I were seeing what was happening, rather than being part of it, seeing for the very first time what had been around me all my life. Pain and grief and sorrow and loss. Brutality. What had happened to me? Was I under a spell? Weakened by the amulet of Usha's claws that should have made me stronger?

One of our enemies tried to pull me from my mare, and I pushed him off, nothing more. I could have used Io's scythe, I could have spilled his blood, chopped him in two, but instead I watched him run, and I felt something I shouldn't have.

Pity. Mercy.

Those burning things.

Our people captured six of their men, killed many, and chased whoever was left to the borders of our land. It didn't matter if they sneaked back for their tents and belongings; they would not bother us for a very long time. They would dream of bees and of women who were half-horse, and they would stay where they belonged: away from us.

The nights were colder, and it was cold as we rode home. I heard my sisters' war cries of victory, but I was silent. Tonight would be the night of the festival. No one who hadn't killed three men would be allowed go. I had killed at least the two I'd seen go down, and surely some others, but when Asteria rode up beside me to ask how many, I said I hadn't killed any.

I didn't want to go to the festival. I wasn't interested in knowing anything about men. I knew enough already. More than enough.

I knew Melek.

Then you'll have to stay home with the children. Asteria laughed. *Even if you do think you're fierce as a bear.*

I washed the dust from my mare when we got home. There was the single drop of blood on her forehead. I fed Sky and let her drink from the stream and then I asked her for guidance. She was quiet and calm, and I took that to mean *Do nothing. Say nothing. Not now.*

Io and I watched the women get ready. Our sisters bathed in the stream, then covered themselves with cinnabar and chalk. They combed their hair with honey. They wore bone jewelry, and the few who had beads wore them as well. Every girl who had recently become a woman and was at the festival for the first time was given more koumiss to drink than the others. The priestesses had their needles ready: Each girl, now turned a woman, was honored by a tattoo at the base of her neck, the blue line of our people.

They let the men view the ritual bath. The fools were entranced by what they'd drank and what they'd smoked and what they saw. Did they not think that there were few men alive who would go on living after being allowed to witness such things? Did they think these women who'd fought so hard were about to become their wives? To cook their meals and sew their clothing and take them into their arms at night?

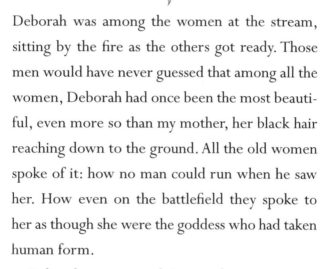

Deborah was among the women at the stream, sitting by the fire as the others got ready. Those men would have never guessed that among all the women, Deborah had once been the most beautiful, even more so than my mother, her black hair reaching down to the ground. All the old women spoke of it: how no man could run when he saw her. How even on the battlefield they spoke to her as though she were the goddess who had taken human form.

Deborah saw me with Io, watching our sisters become more and more beautiful. She saw the look on my face as I studied the fire. Deborah motioned to me to come to her. You can never deny a priestess anything, and I should have gone to her, but instead I grabbed Io's hand and ran away.

You can't be afraid of the fire, Io teased me. *What did you see there? A spirit? A demon?*

I didn't say that it was myself that I saw in that fire. I was there, in every blue flame, riding away, farther than I'd ever gone before, alone.

Are you sorry you're not going? Io asked me later, when the sky was turning dark. We were in our tent, under our blanket, when the festival began, but we could hear them. There was drumming and what sounded like war cries. It was the mystery of the goddess that was being revealed, but I didn't want to see it.

The men had already been taken to the priestesses and given a mixture of koumiss and hemp. By now they probably thought they were dreaming. They would not protest as they were dressed up like stags by the old women. Each man would wear the pelt of a stag, and a headdress with long horns. Their faces would be painted with ochre and yellow dust until they themselves wouldn't know who they were.

Against my back, Io shivered.

Will they kill them? she asked me.

When they're done with them, most likely.

Some men were set free, some were kept, like the smith we had among us. There were people who believed that the bear in the sky was made up of the skulls of seven smiths, killed by our grandmothers, but still watching over us. It was a cruel time, and we knew that; still, we had to go on, otherwise our people would disappear, like a drop of blood on the earth, vanishing into the yellow clay.

We could hear the wild songs in our dreams. Our people were drinking mares' milk and taking out their carved pipes to smoke hemp; they had covered their bodies with a paste made out of the red flowers that grew on the steppes. They were dreaming, too, only they were still awake. It was the trance state, for one and all. It was the way we had always done things. It was for the sake of our daughters-to-be.

This was the way our people were made, daughters formed from battle and joy, not from sorrow, the way I had been. As for the men, they thought they were in heaven, a deep heaven of dreams they had never imagined. Our people were upon them, not with weapons this time, but with their own bodies, covered with ochre and honey.

My dreams were different. In my tent, I was dreaming of the black horse. I was running beside it, through the snow. I could feel my own breath, the billow of heat in the frozen air. I could hear the horse, his hooves, his breath. I reached him and grabbed his mane, then lifted myself up. There was a pounding in my head, the echo of horses' hooves. *Wait for me, brother,* I said to the horse, but he was too fast and he threw me and in my dream I was falling.

I awoke falling, startled, and in her sleep, Io held on to me. But it wasn't enough. My dream felt more real than my own tent. I went outside, into the cold morning. I could indeed see my breath in the air. It was so quiet, there weren't even any birds. I could smell last night's fires burning out and the odor of hemp. It looked as though a battle had been fought right here in our city. There were women sleeping outside, unprotected from the cold, still in the last grip of their trance. I saw two men, far on the steppe, wearing nothing, running like deer. The others I didn't want to see.

I thought I saw my mother among the women who had been to the festival, but that was impossible. She already had her daughter, her Queen-to-be.

But if I was to be the Queen, why was it that I wanted to be gone from this place? Why was I thinking of the grass that grew so tall, the hillock above Melek's city of tents?

I took my horse and rode north. I rode for the sake of riding, to be my mare's sister, but there was something more in what I did. I knew that when I passed the place where Usha had been killed. Where her blood had seeped out, the ground was darker now, more black than red. I got down and walked a circle, begging for my sister-bear's protection. And then I saw something white gleaming. I bent down and there was a bear tooth. I held it in my hands, then got on my knees and thanked Usha for watching over me, the way the bear in the sky watches over all of our people.

I took the leather strand that held Io's seashell from around my neck, then chiseled a small hole in the ridge of Usha's tooth with my knife and threaded the leather through. The tooth felt good around my neck, as though I had found the bear inside of Usha. Inside of me.

I rode on. I wanted to take a look, nothing more. When I got to the bluff Melek's city was there, but it was abandoned. His people had already gone on, toward some higher ground where they could last the winter. I rode down into their city. I had nothing to fear from emptiness.

I left my mare and went inside a tent. It smelled of food and smoke. Some cooking things had been left behind, and a stone anvil used by a smith. I went to another tent, then another. I felt I was knowing these people from standing in their homes. I was interested. But really, I was something else, too. I wanted to know what was beyond my own people. It was curiosity, that dangerous thing. It was something opening inside me.

I knew I had found Melek's tent because he had left something behind. Maybe he knew me better than I'd ventured to guess; maybe he knew I would come here. Propped up near the place where a fire had once burned, there was an image of a bear carved in stone. It was a flat stone, no bigger than my hand, carefully wrought. When I looked closely I saw that the bear had my face, and that the face was beautiful.

I rode home; I wanted to be back before dark. Our people were packing up, dismantling their tents. It would soon be time to go to the winter-lands, everyone knew that. I turned my mare to trot toward my tent; I hoped no one would notice me. But all at once every dog in our city began to bark. They were turned to me, barking, as if they could see what no human could see: that the Angel of Death rode beside me.

The Queen must have heard those dogs. That night she called me to her tent. I was shaking at the thought of appearing before my mother.

Alina and Penthe sat close together as I came inside, my head lowered out of respect. Penthe asked me to eat with them, some of the mares' meat from the night festival. I said I had already eaten with Io, which was not true.

I was too nervous to eat in front of the Queen.

I sat down across from them, my head still bowed.

The Queen wore a coat made of horsehide, fastened with brass buckles. She looked beautiful. I could hardly believe she was indeed my mother.

We're hoping you will soon have a sister, the Queen said.

I looked up and saw there were lines of ochre paint on her face.

I have a sister, I said. *Io.*

Penthe reached across and touched my hand, grateful.

A blood sister, my Queen said.

Now I understood that my mother had indeed been at the festival. The only reason for her to be with a man was to bring forth a second daughter, a Queen. I did not please her or satisfy her. She wanted a different daughter, a different Queen. Now that it was out in the open the sorrow floated between us. I was Rain to her and nothing more. Someone she wanted to forget.

I lifted my head so I could look at my mother, and as I expected she looked away. So I bowed my head again.

By this time you should have killed enough men to become a woman, my mother told me. *We will see how brave your sister is.*

My sister Io is quite brave, I said in a quiet voice. For this there was no argument.

Thank you, Penthe said to me, acknowledging only what was true.

We will see who this blood sister of yours is when she arrives, my mother said.

I looked at the Queen and this time she didn't look away. I should have been angry, furious, hurt. I should have said, *Why is it you can only see sorrow when you see me when I am so much more! Why do you only see rain?*

Instead I said what any of our people would have said to our Queen.

Whatever you wish. I am your servant in this and all things.

Soon enough our people knew that my mother would have another daughter, and that once she arrived I would no longer be the Queen-to-be. Now when I walked through our city no one bothered to stop speaking in my honor. I heard some girls laughing at me. When I went to practice with the warriors, Asteria took me aside. She who had endless courage, who had killed so many of our enemy there wasn't room on her quiver to make another red mark, looked down her nose at me. She no longer pretended to like me.

If you had wanted to be an archer you should have

made that decision when the time came, Asteria said. *It's too late for you to be a true warrior.*

I had become nothing, not even something-to-be. I was no longer allowed to go to battle with the elite, but instead I was left to trail behind with the girls who were too young or too weak, once again helping the priestesses who cared for the dead.

Deborah called me to her, and I had no choice but to go. We were nearly ready for the move to higher ground. The horses knew this and were restless. I went to the place where the priestesses lived. There were ravens pecking at the ground, looking for answers to their questions.

I have something for you, Deborah said.

Why? I'm worthless.

Maybe that's what you want to believe.

I raised my eyes, angry.

Why would I want to believe such a thing? You know what my Queen's decision is. I'm like drops of water in her eyes.

If she doesn't see who you are, she will lose everything. Don't do the same. Make your own fortune.

The priestess offered me a drink of honey and mares' milk and something else, something to protect me, an herb she had never even given to her own daughter. I took the horn that held the mixture and drank it all. Now when I looked into the fire I could see the priestess herself. I thought she was beside me, but no, when I looked into the fire she was there.

She held up her hands and the black horse that was galloping toward her stopped.

It's right in front of you, I said.

We both knew I was seeing Deborah's death. She was so old and weak that when a raven came to perch on her knee the priestess no longer had the strength to wave it away. I pulled one of its feathers and it flew off, cawing. When Deborah turned to me I saw there was a cloud of white over her eyes. She could see what was inside a person, but she could no longer see the outside. I could see the breath of the black horse when she breathed out.

The high priestess honored me by whispering to me a great secret, meant for my ears alone.

She sees only rain when she looks at you, but even a Queen can be wrong. You are the prophecy. You're what's to come.

All that falling leaf season I helped get the horses ready for the journey to the winterlands. I liked the work I did, caring for the horses, keeping them calm when the smith fit their bridles. Because I had inherited my great-grandmother's talent, I could think the way they did. I knew when they were thirsty. When they were hungry, I knew to bring them hay. Io helped me. I could feel her fear lessening. One day I saw her atop the roan horse that had been given to her as a gift by our Queen, chosen by Penthe because of its color, a red sister for red-haired Io.

The horse looked startled at first, but Io wrapped her hands in its mane and whispered something to it and the mare began to trot. Then, all at once, the roan mare began to run.

I leapt onto the horse I was grooming, Asteria's big yellow mare, and chased after Io. The trees were dropping their needles on the ground. The wind was bitter. I caught up with my sister at last, and used my leather belt to catch the roan horse around its neck, slow it, then stop it.

Now I saw that Io was laughing. Her face was flushed.

This is what I've been missing! Why didn't you tell me it felt like flying in the wind?

We rode back together and I felt lucky to have a sister. Maybe I would feel lucky yet again when my new sister was born. I was free now, really. But even if I was no longer the Queen-to-be I still felt the burden of something else. The prophecy.

Io and I found the bridle and the stirrups the smith had once made for her.

He said you'd never ride. I laughed. Perhaps a foretelling could be wrong.

When we began to travel to higher ground, Io no longer followed along with the old women and children, coughing in the dust raised by a thousand horses. But she was slower than the warriors. I kept pace alongside her. In the past, I had ridden to the winterlands out in front alongside Asteria and Astella's archers, and our people looked different from where I was now. For miles there was a yellow storm cloud rising into the cold blue air, as if our people were a line of color, a drop of red blood on the yellow earth. At first, it looked as though our people stretched on forever, but when we reached the higher ground and the mountains appeared you could tell where we stopped and the rest of the earth began.

The mountains were already coated with snow, and from this distance they looked purple and blue. That was winter in front of us. We still had some time to hunt and get ready for what was to come. We had time to move into the caves. I thought of Usha who was now inside me. Her tooth on my leather necklace, her claws packed inside my horsehide bag along with my heavy shirt for winter made of hide and hair, and the stone carving that reminded me of who I was and who I might be. The bear with my face. The gift I'd been given.

The reminder of who I was inside.

In the House

IN THE HOUSE OF MY MOTHER it was too
silent.

Winter had come and stayed for a very long time.
The snow fell more deeply than anyone could remember. We were in the caves below the mountains. Asteria and Astella and their warriors had
set their tents out in the open, to protect us, but
soon even they had to come inside the caves. The

world was dark and it was bright. Black inside, blinding white outside.

Our horses were kept in the pastureland below, but soon they could not move; they were trapped in the drifts. We had to go and chop away at the snow with axes, then hack through the icy stream so that they could drink. All through the cooling weather we had cut grass. Now we lined the caves with it, food for our sisters, warm beds for ourselves. But the food became less and less and we had to kill some of our own sister-horses, or they would have starved. We thanked their spirits as we ate them, as we sewed the clothes we made from them and braided together their long tail hair for thread.

Deborah and the priestesses were off by themselves in a small cave where we left offerings. Meat and milk they could warm on their fire. Blankets made of newly tanned horsehide. Every time I went to give the offerings, Deborah seemed smaller. In her black clothes she looked like a raven herself with her black eyes and her beak of a nose and all of those blue lines tattooed on her face that told the story of her life. She had been an archer once, and had burned off her left breast. She had been so young and beautiful men had wept at the sight of her. Now she was a raven waiting for me to bring her mares' milk to drink.

Don't you want your fortune told? she'd ask whenever I came to the cave.

We would both laugh then. A black joke we shared, for the augury was what I wanted least of all. My own fortune terrified me. My fate frightened me more than the high snowdrifts.

Don't be afraid of the foretelling, she whispered. *It's the way the world should be.*

We had brought the bees with us, and the caves buzzed from the logs in which they lived. At night, they beat their wings to keep the honey at the right temperature. It froze anyway, and many of the bees froze as well; those that remained went to sleep, as the bears do, as we try to do, outdistancing the winter with dreams.

Io and I still took care of the horses. We would cover ourselves with horsehide until we were sister-horses, unrecognizable as human beings, then we'd trudge through the snow with hay on our shoulders and in our hair. Now I realize that we were happy. Though we were freezing, though our stomachs growled. We would hold hands and spin around in the snow until we fell down. The horses would run to us as though we were the guardians of their spirits. People laughed at me when we came back, sweating and exhausted. My work was not a proper job for a Queen-to-be, but that was someone else anyway. That was my sister who had not yet arrived.

My mother was big with her baby, as were the other women who had been with men at the festival. But my mother was more uncomfortable than the other women, vomiting much of what she ate. At night, she moaned and could not sleep. Maybe the new Queen couldn't wait to be born and was kicking to be free. My mother had picked the best warrior from among the men, the most handsome, the strongest — no one else could have him — and afterward had set him free to run home like a deer. All she wanted was his seed, not his life. Just to start her daughter inside her, my sister the Queen. But he must have planted something else as well, because when the snow was at its highest, our Queen became feverish, burning hot to the touch.

Cybelle made her sister mixtures of honey and milk, but the Queen could not even keep that down. My mother's stomach was huge, but she could not eat. She was starving like some of our mares, even though she was brought food enough for three people.

I knew how bad this illness was when I saw the look on Penthe's face. She sat at the mouth of the cave looking out at the falling snow, her complexion as white as the world outside. We knew she was weeping without seeing her face, even though she didn't make a sound. The daughters from the festival were not supposed to be born until it was nearly spring, and yet my mother seemed already racked with the pain of a woman whose child is fighting to be born.

One morning, Penthe came to me and woke me. Io and I were sleeping side by side to keep each other warm, beneath the same blanket. When I looked up I thought for a minute it was Io who was staring at me, panicked, the white face, the red hair, then I saw the familiar red henna tattoos on Penthe's face and the tears.

I need you to go to the priestesses, she told me. *Find out what I have to do to make your mother well.*

Penthe had never asked anything of me, or of anyone. There was a storm outside, but I got dressed quickly and pulled on my horsehide boots and my thickest shirt. I had to walk slowly, breaking up the snow before me with my axe. Snow got inside me when I breathed and it threaded through my dark hair, turning it white, as though I'd been made old, but I kept on. Stones had been placed at the mouth of the priestesses' cave to keep animals out, and I climbed over them. I had worn my bear claws to keep me warm, and when the priestesses saw me they backed away, thinking I was a beast.

It's only me, I said.

But they didn't seem to hear. They were chanting together, and one of them threw a bit of magic into the fire. The flame rose up, redder, brighter, like the sun. Then they saw me and knew me for who I was. Not a bear, but a sister to the bear.

I found Deborah lying in her blankets on the far side of the fire. Her hands had become stiff, a raven's talons. I drank some of the warm mares' milk I was offered and held the drinking horn to Deborah's lips.

My mother the Queen needs help, I said.

I told Deborah that the Queen couldn't eat and was wasting away. She seemed ready for her daughter to come even though it was still winter.

Deborah gathered her strength and made me a package of herbs. They smelled fresh, like spring.

She'll be able to eat if she takes this. But there's something else she needs to do.

I didn't like the sound of this. Deborah's breathing was raspy, and she sounded worried. I thought she had seen everything, knew everything, in this world and the next, and that nothing could frighten her. She came close so she could whisper, so the other priestesses would not hear.

She has to let him live.

Penthe was waiting for me in the snow. Her fingers and face were turning blue from the cold and there was snow in her hair. She was pacing back and forth, desperate. I gave her the packet of herbs and followed her as she rushed to my mother's chamber.

The best blankets were on the floor, made of red thread and white horsehide. There was a fire to keep the cave warm. The Queen was shivering, her eyes closed. Her dark skin looked ashy. When she opened her eyes I wasn't sure she recognized Penthe.

Your daughter brought something to save you, Penthe said.

My daughter? The Queen's voice sounded far away, as though it had been carried by the wind. *She's not yet born.*

Penthe turned to me. *She doesn't know what she's saying. Don't listen to her.*

I understood why my mother loved Penthe then. Penthe's heart was unlike any other; it was large enough to include even me.

Penthe made a tea of the herbs. I sat beside the Queen; she was sweating as though it were still summer. I reached and touched my mother's face, something I'd never done before. Her flesh burned me.

That feels so good, the Queen murmured. *Like rain.*

Help me lift her head, Penthe said. Together we did so and my mother drank the herbs through her parched lips.

Penthe and I watched as my mother tossed and turned, then fell asleep.

She'll be all right now, Penthe said. *Strong again.*

But Penthe's face wasn't as sure as her words. The henna tattoos of snakes seemed to move in the firelight.

She will be, I agreed, and Penthe looked at me with gratitude.

In return she gave me something I had never expected. She took my hands in hers.

It's not that she doesn't want you to be the Queen. It's that you don't want it.

I didn't say anything to that. I felt as though I'd been slapped. How could my mother know what I wanted when I didn't know myself?

That night when I went to check on the horses, I told Io to stay behind. It was too cold for her. In the sky, the great bear's tail was to the north. Everything seemed far away and cold. I had not told Penthe the priestess's message, and my mother was too ill to hear. But I was born with the taste of prophecy in my mouth, the bitter taste of the laurel, and I knew what was to come. I sank to my knees and asked Usha's spirit for guidance, but all I heard was the silence of the snow and the horses coming toward me, invisible with all the white flakes that covered

them until they were upon me, my sisters, each
and every one.

Io came for me when I was out with the horses,
spreading out what was left of the hay. I knew the
time was near. Io's eyes were bright with tears. She
didn't have to say the Queen was worsening. I ran
back following in Io's footsteps. I was shaking
when I went to see my mother. For a little while
the tea the priestess had sent had helped her; she
had drank some mares' milk and the sweat had disappeared from her face. But that relief hadn't
lasted. Now she was worse, stone cold, wrapped
in blankets. She could barely sit up. Leaning against
the wall was her painted wooden quiver, marked
from battle, marked by her strength. But she was
weaker than ever. She was fading in front of us.

I knelt beside her and it took a while for the
Queen's eyes to find me. She recognized me
right away.

Did the priestess have any message for me? the
Queen asked.

I had never seen her this way. It was fear I saw inside her. I thought about the girl she had been when the fifty had attacked her. I thought she must have looked like this, different from the woman she'd become. For an instant, I felt I knew her. I wanted to protect her, just this once.

The priestess said nothing, I told her. *Only that you should rest and be well.*

The Queen studied me to see whether or not she should believe me.

I gave you the wrong name, she said.

I felt something hot in my eyes that I knew could not be tears. Could she see that I was something more than sorrow? Could I see that as well?

I should have waited to name you until I knew you. I should have known you before now.

I thanked the Queen and kissed her hand. *I'm Rain, and I'm grateful for that name.*

Her hand was too cold even for this cold time.

What can I do for you? I whispered.

But she had already closed her eyes, and Penthe told me she needed her strength for other things. What those things were neither of us wanted to know or say or even think about. But here is what I saw before I walked away: I saw my mother's shadow, resting there beside her. It had returned to her after all this time.

It was late at night when it happened. Dream-time, a bad hour for things of this world. When it came, it was horrible. Worse than men dying, worse than women fighting. Blood against blood. Bone against bone. They gathered the other women who would soon have daughters and took them deep into the caves so they would not fret or panic and then lose their own daughters due to fear. But the screaming followed them, with a jagged edge, like wind. It was impossible to escape such things. It was death from the inside out.

The baby was coming too soon. It had happened before to other women, but not to our Queen, my mother. All of the women who knew how to bring daughters into this word had been summoned. They made my mother walk, even though she was so weak, to try to stop the baby from coming.

We need the priestess, Penthe told me.

She looked as ill as the Queen, pale, shaking, but she thought of my mother first, as she always had. She sent me to get Deborah. I didn't bother with my heaviest shirts; I just pulled on my boots and ran. There was a crust of ice over the snow and I ran fast, flying. But Deborah could not come with me. She was too old to get there in time. She could barely move out of her blankets. I knew from her expression that she had no hope. All the same, she sent her daughter, Greeya, with me. Greeya was wise in the ways of babies and she was quick. I could barely keep up with her as we ran across the ice.

We could hear the Queen wailing before we got there. Her voice was shaking the branches in the trees, and then it stopped. We ran faster. Most of the women who knew how to bring forth daughters were on their knees, praying to the goddess for guidance. Greeya sat down and had Penthe lift my mother's blankets and her clothes so she could reach inside the Queen. This was a birth that had gone wrong; there was too much blood, not enough time, nothing anyone could do. My mother screamed like a warrior. And then, like a woman in pain.

I could not watch that. I turned away. I covered my ears with my hands.

Greeya murmured that one life was being lit while another was burning out at the very same time.

Then kill it, I heard Penthe say. *Maybe that will save her. Do anything!*

But it was too late. The baby was already being born. The Queen was already dying.

Greeya helped to bring the baby out into the light, this child who was meant to be Queen. She quickly untangled it and cleared out its mouth with one finger.

All I could hear was Penthe, raging, weeping. She threw herself across Alina until there was as much blood on her as there was on my mother.

It was silent again, everywhere, except for Penthe's sobbing. I turned and saw the spirit leave my mother, a cloud of air rising from her pale lips. I saw the look on Greeya's face and I knew.

My brother had arrived in this world.

Kill it, Penthe said.

Asteria and Astella and my mother's sister, Cybelle, came to kneel and honor the Queen. They all echoed Penthe's words. But I remembered what Deborah had said. Greeya picked up the baby that had made us lose our Queen and tucked it inside her shirt. I led her back to the mouth of the cave, then I stopped her.

Don't kill him, I said.

You heard what they told me! And it's not for you to tell a priestess what should be. Lead me back!

Bring him to Deborah, and do what I say or I'll find you and send you to the next world. Do it!

Greeya looked at me in a different way. She nodded, though I knew she didn't want to.

Penthe and Io prepared the Queen for the next world. They washed her hair with melted stream water, then plaited it with honey. They bathed her body and covered it with a fine film of honey to protect her skin. Two golden bracelets were placed upon her arms. A dozen of the best warriors sat together and stitched a death blanket for the Queen, the finest there was, with horsehair thread from her own beloved horse. Then Cybelle and the bee women wrapped the Queen in half a dozen blankets, bound with leather and brass bells.

All through the caves women who had no fear of any man sat weeping.

Asteria and Astella rode my mother's great war horse, Pearl, into the catacombs where our Queens are buried, the largest kurgan, the burial mounds made in the time of our great-grandmothers. The kurgan rose like a mountain at the edge of the pasture, covered with blue ice and snow. The archers rode into the kurgan at the secret opening, and then they killed the Queen's horse, weeping as they did. This was our holy ground, a catacomb so wide across it was like a bowl made for the goddess. Along with the Queen's horse Asteria and Astella buried all of my mother's weapons, her bronze mirror, her rings, her whet-stone for sharpening knives and axes, her carved bone spoon, fourteen amulets given to her by our fourteen priestesses.

The priestesses all came; they carried Deborah and chanted for an entire night and then a day and through another night. They ate the ritual horse-meat that had been coated with herbs; they covered their bodies with the paste from the red flowers and sat in a trance. With one foot in this world and one in the world to come they could help my mother move into the next world accompanied by those who loved her.

Because Penthe was not of our people, she was not allowed to join the mystery. She sat outside the catacomb, dragging her fingernails across her face until she was bleeding. I told her when I went inside I would say a prayer for my mother in her name. Penthe grabbed my hand, but she did not speak. I had no choice but to leave her, and go in-side the kurgan.

In honor of my mother, I tore my finest shirt. I painted my face with the yellow earth. Then I sat before the priestesses and had four blue lines tattooed on my face, without first drinking koumiss. I didn't cry out, not once. I brought my treasured bear claws to place beside my mother, so that Usha would find Alina in the next world and protect her. When I went to place my gift beside my mother, everyone took a step away and bowed their heads, and then I understood. Because my sister had not come, they had no choice but to do so.

I was now the Queen.

The edges of the snow had begun to melt in the bright light of the last day of our mourning. But it was cold, too cold for Penthe to be outside weeping. Io took her mother back to the cave; I had other things to do. I went with the priestesses, helping to carry Deborah. When the high priestess was beneath her blanket, and the others couldn't hear, I asked for him. My brother.

Deborah clucked her tongue and drew her dark cloak around her shoulders. *He's weak. Weak babies don't last. He's been alone for three days.*

If you can keep him till the snow melts I'll bring him to his father's people.

If I go on feeding him with mares' milk the way I've been doing, I warn you. It will make him strong, the priestess told me. *It will make your heart strong for him as well.*

Here was my secret: I wanted him to be strong. I wanted him to live.

When I could finally get away I went to see him. He was in a little cavern that had been chipped into the cave long ago by melting ice. He'd been wrapped in a blanket and he knew enough not to cry. There was a bit of blanket soaked in mares' milk for him to suck on. He stared right at me, unafraid. Like me, he had yellow eyes. His hair was black, like mine.

Deborah had dragged herself out of her blanket. She was watching us. We were never to name boy babies, for they wouldn't be with us long. They would be disposed of, or given back to the people from which they had come. Name something, and it belongs to you. Everyone knew that.

But I went against the rules.

Anto, I said. It was our word for black horse.

Deborah nodded. She knew I had chosen the right name for my brother. She did not berate me for breaking the rules.

He's the one you dreamt, the priestess said. *Now your fortune is upon you.*

In the

Age

IN THE AGE OF WOMANHOOD you cannot know what will happen. You were one thing as a girl, but who will you become? I had been rain, sorrow, the sister of the bear, the keeper of the horses, and now I was the Queen. We traveled back to our spring pastures, our summerlands. Slowly, in grief for all we had lost. We left behind our Queen and our highest priestess, cared for by her daughter, since Deborah was unable to complete the journey. We left behind the horses that had not made it through the hardest winter in memory. We left behind who we had been when we'd been in service to our Queen. But we were coming back to the summerlands with twelve new daughters, all bundled into blankets that were tied to their mothers' backs.

●━━━━━━━━➤

It took us nearly a month to make this journey. And in this time I saw Astella and Asteria whispering to each other, arguing, I think. But I never could tell for certain; they always made themselves quiet whenever I was near. My aunt, Cybelle, rode beside me, to give me her blessing and try to stop the talk that I was not my mother's daughter, not the one she'd had in mind as the leader for her people.

Let them buzz, Cybelle whispered. *Just like the bees. Soon enough they'll stop and go about their business.*

Io rode with her mother, for Penthe couldn't be trusted not to flee and wander back the way we'd come. She had refused to leave the Queen.

When we left, we'd had to drag her away from the catacombs and tie her with rope to the neck of her horse. Even now, Io had to keep a close eye on her mother.

In front of us the pastures were green, like a sea. I rode standing up, to honor my mother's spirit. We built our city of tents as soon as we arrived in good pastureland, and mine went in the place of the rightful Queen. That night, before anyone rested or ate, I was bathed in mares' milk and a huge platter of meat was set before me. I was given new boots and a new shirt, one the young girls had been working on since the Queen had died. People lowered their eyes when they spoke to me, but I could tell, all wasn't well. There were rumors and a division amongst us. The archers stayed off by themselves. They did not offer me their allegiance or sit beside me. They never once called me their Queen.

One night Penthe came to me. She bowed as though I were truly the Queen and I asked her not to do so. She was Penthe, and I was Rain, neither needed to bow to the other. All the same,

Penthe wasn't the same as she had been; her hair had turned white and her red henna tattoos were fading. She had one foot in the spirit world searching for her beloved Queen and the other foot in our world.

They say you haven't even killed three men, Penthe said.

I haven't killed three, I've killed six. The four who killed Usha, my bear, and two in my first battle.

Penthe nodded, understanding I had not told anyone about this because I had not wanted to attend the festival.

Well, then they say you haven't killed the boy.

Penthe was looking directly into my face. It was the time of bees and there were logs all over our city filled with the Queen bee's servants, each one dripping honey. The air was sweet, but now it was cloying. Too much. Too sweet.

What boy? My chest hurt with my deceit.

You need to get rid of him. Otherwise there might be a king someday who wants a thousand wives to serve him.

That will never happen, I said.

Send him to the next world. Penthe had a huge heart, but not for this boy, my brother the black horse. *And let everyone know that's what you're doing. You'll be no one's Queen until you make this sacrifice.*

—————▶

There was a gathering on the first full moon since we'd come to the pasturelands. I covered my face with ochre and chalk. I dressed in my finest clothes. I painted my mare yellow and red, my mother's favorite colors. I came to the meeting with every weapon I had been given as the new Queen, all strapped to my back with rope.

I am going off to kill the boy, my brother, who killed the Queen. This is what you expect of me, and this is what I intend to do.

My aunt Cybelle came to embrace me. A war cry went up and I felt that cry in my blood.

We will wait for you, Cybelle said.

But Asteria came riding up.

You're so ready to be the Queen, Asteria said. *But once you said it wouldn't suit you. Perhaps you'd like another who's more sure of herself to step forward.*

Even Astella looked at Asteria, shocked by her nerve.

I'm sure of myself, I said. At that moment I was. I knew what I was about to do. I had already made choices I hadn't expected; the decisions of a Queen.

My archers would like to come with you. To serve you, of course. In case you say you'll get rid of the child, and then change your mind, we will be there in your place.

If you don't trust me enough to do it, why should I trust you enough to accompany me?

The archers looked at each other; there was no answer for that.

No, I'll leave myself in the morning.

⬝━━━➤

That night as I was getting ready, Io came to me and said she would go with me. To protect me, she said. My sister who had never been in battle, never lifted the scythe I'd had made for her until she gave it back to me.

Stay here and take care of Penthe.

Then let me sing to you so you can sleep and be re-freshed for your journey, Io insisted.

My sister wrapped her arms around me and sang me to sleep, the song from the north storm country whose words I didn't understand. Maybe that was why I woke in the middle of the night. Or maybe it was my dream of the black horse calling to me. I would not bother to wait for morning. I would let the dark cover me, and make certain I rode alone.

I sneaked out so as not to wake Io. I covered her with my blankets so she would not be cold without me, then I packed up my weapons, went for my horse, and left.

We raced across the grasslands; I didn't let my mare rest until we neared the place where my bear had been killed. I got off my horse to honor Usha before I went on. When I went onto my knees I found the last of Usha's teeth in the circle where the grass still did not grow. I gathered them into a leather pouch and tied the pouch to my waist. Now that I was Queen I didn't braid my hair, but let it fall loose down my back. I had been given four more lines of blue on each of my cheeks, for courage, for protection, for wisdom, for luck.

I thought about Melek, how close his village was, and I wondered if his people had returned. But there was little time to wonder and I knew I shouldn't be thinking about him; I rode hard the rest of the way. When I reached the priestesses' cave, I tied up my mare, spoke a blessing, and entered into the darkness.

It still felt like winter inside the cave, though there was a fire. Greeya came to me and bowed her head. Her eyes looked red with some foretold sorrow.

How is our priestess? I asked.

Still in this world, but only because she's waiting for you.

I wasn't surprised that the high priestess knew I was coming. She likely understood before I did that I would have to make this journey. I went to pay my respects. I'd brought Deborah a comb made of bone for her hair, since even now she was vain, though her hair was snow white; and I'd brought her a bundle of deer meat that would give her strength. We dined together and then I asked for the Black Horse, Anto.

I told you he was too weak to live, Deborah said.

My face must have betrayed me because she laughed.

But I made him strong. He's in his place.

Anto was in his nook in the wall, bundled in a blanket. I could hear him making noises, more like a dove than a horse. When I reached for him, he looked at me carefully with his yellow eyes. He was staring at me as though he knew me, perhaps from another life, perhaps from a world-to-be.

Deborah was weaker than ever, but she dragged herself over. She sat beside me as I held the baby. *Mares' milk can make a baby into a king,* Deborah said, considering what we'd done.

They want me to kill him. And he's a baby now. Nothing more.

That's what I did to mine. I looked at Deborah, but she didn't seem to notice. *When I had a son I had no choice. It was our way.*

The priestess was shaking with the tremor of old age, but also with something more.

It still is, I said.

Is it?

I looked at Deborah and saw the girl she had been, long before she became a priestess, when her hair was black and reached to the earth. He had been her first child, this son of hers, there in the time when she had no choice. She said she'd done it gently, not the way other women did, leaving baby boys on the steppes for the wolves and the ravens. She'd covered his face and sang to him. She'd been with him when his spirit went on. Even still, she dreamed of him every night.

It may still be our way, but don't all ways change, for bad and for good? the priestess asked me. *Take a single arrowhead from those scattered around your mother. That will be the foretelling. It will show you the way.*

I thought about my own dreams, how in that deep nightworld it was always my duty to run with the Black Horse, not to trap or kill him. I held my brother close. He smelled like mares' milk and horses. Just a baby. He studied my face.

Maybe he was surprised to see yellow eyes, so much like his.

I thought if there was anyone who could tell me what to do it was my mother. I rode to the catacombs, to the secret entrance, and moved away enough rocks to fit through into the chamberway. Since it was pitch-black I took a torch with me; even with the torch, I could hardly remember the way to my mother's resting place. Straight, and then two turns, Deborah had told me, but I circled, lost.

It was hushed and freezing cold beneath the earth. At last I came to the place of my great-grandmother, the Queen who had first spoken to horses. I crept over the rocks that kept my great-grandmother safe from prowlers, then I got down on my knees and sang to her. The bones of her beloved horse had been buried with her, and five other horses as well. The blankets she'd been wrapped in had all been dyed a deep blue, the color of our people. I took the leather pouch from around my waist and took the bear's teeth to leave for her, all but the one I wore around my neck.

Thank you, I said to my great-grandmother. *For speaking to horses, for being my grandmother, for showing me the way.*

I climbed back past the rocks and went on until I found my mother. The earth was streaked dark and light outside her resting place, as if Penthe's tears had reached here. I thought of the look on my mother's face that day when I brought her the priestess's herbs, how frightened she'd been, and I did not blame her for naming me Rain or for turning away from me.

If I don't deserve to be the Queen, then I will go away, I told my mother. *I will respect your wishes.*

I waited there for a long while, hoping she would send me a message from the next world. I sang to her, the song Io had taught me, whose words I still didn't understand. I liked how comforting it was. I liked the sound of it, sister to sister, daughter to mother.

The blankets around the Queen were made of felt, the finest ever made, dyed blue in the way of our people. I took one of the arrowheads that had belonged to my mother, as Deborah had told me to do. There were scores of bronze ones, but only one that was yellow. I took that one.

If you wish me to be rid of my brother I will use your arrowhead, I told the Queen. *I will be in service to you always, in all things.*

I went back to the priestesses' cave in the dark. Greeya had supper ready and I sat beside Deborah.

What did you decide? the old priestess asked.

Is there a right and a wrong? I needed to know.

There's a done and an undone. You need to ask yourself this: Do you wish to dream of the black horse all your life?

⟶

I went to where the baby was. He was asleep, yellow eyes closed. I had the arrowhead in my hand. It felt hot. In the dark it looked golden. So yellow it was like sunlight. What I would have done I am not sure, and I never will be, because the arrowhead began to shift as though it were melting in my hand. When I looked down I saw that the metal had bent at the edge.

Greeya had come up behind me. *You took the gold one.* She clapped her hands. *Deborah said you would. It's the only arrowhead that's not strong enough to pierce through human flesh. It's your answer,* she said.

Because of that my brother lived. The priest-esses packed up his milk rags, a horn of mares' milk, his blanket sewn with black thread, and the leather strapping I looped over my shoulders so I could carry him close to my chest as I rode.

I went east, beyond where we'd fought the people of Black Horse's father. It was far past the bound-aries of our lands, for we'd chased them all the way to the Black Sea. It took several days to get there, and Anto was as good as any baby could be. My brother did not cry much, only when he was hungry, and I fed him as we rode. He was alive, no dream. Just a baby, nothing more, Black Horse, and he stared at me as he sucked his mares' milk. I tried not to look at him. He was something I should not have named if I didn't want to care for him, a good baby with yellow eyes.

I tracked Anto's father's people until there was salt in the air. Salt clung to my horse and to me. Anto's father's people had become beach people and had built a city out of stones and shells. I waited on the higher ground above the shoreline, hidden by shrubs, until a boy came by. The boy stumbled into my trap, the sort you make for birds and rabbits. He was so startled he didn't move when I appeared from the bushes and cut him down from the net. I told him in words and motions to find me the man who'd been taken by the warrior women and who had then returned.

The boy held up two fingers. Of course, there had been two men released that night.

The handsome one was the one I wanted. The strong one. *Only tell him and no one else I am here.*

I waited in the bushes, feeding Black Horse, wondering if a troupe of warriors would come after me and if I'd have to kill them. I heard someone, so I left Black Horse under a thornbush for protection. It was only one man who stood before me. The handsome one. He had stopped a safe distance away.

He let me know his people didn't intend to bother us again.

In return I told him I had a gift for him. *Wait here.* I went to get the baby. *Your son,* I said.

The man made a motion that he didn't understand what I was saying, but I knew that he did. He saw Anto's yellow eyes and mine as well. I wondered if this man might have known the one of the fifty cowards who had been my father.

Take him away, the handsome man told me. He threw his arms in the air as though throwing Black Horse away. *If the baby stays here he'll be killed,* the man told me, haltingly, in my own language. *He has women's blood in him.*

I laughed at what a fool he was. *Every man does.*

Her blood, the handsome man said. He spit on the ground. Then I saw him for who he was. Another coward. Useless. He wasn't worthy of our Queen's child. He wasn't a fighter or a leader or anything worthwhile.

I rode away and didn't look back. I hadn't said my brother's name before; now I called him Anto. He was more than a curse or dream. I sang him the song Io had taught me and he grew quiet.

I would not give him up to just anyone, leave him
to the wolves and the ravens. This was what happened when you named someone: You couldn't
throw him away.

➤━━━━━➤

I stopped at the place where the bear had been
killed. I bowed my head and prayed for guidance.
When I looked up I saw a sign. Perhaps my
mother had sent it to me, perhaps my great-
grandmother, or perhaps the guidance had come
from Usha, who had protected me when she was
in this world and continued to protect me from
the next.

For there was another bear, a tiny cub, smaller
even than Usha had been when I found her. Cubs
are born in time when the world is growing
colder, never in the warming weather, so I wondered if this cub had fallen from the great bear in
the sky. Maybe it was a gift, as Usha had been.

Wherever the cub came from, it was a fierce
thing, male, a brother for Anto. The cub fought
me when I picked it up, but it was starving and
gave up the fight soon enough; it took one of the

milk rags in its mouth and sucked the mares'
milk.

Don't think you are a horse, I told the bear.
Remember what you are.

I took a blanket and tied it round the cub, then
strapped it to my back. Anto opened his yellow
eyes and stared hard at the bear. The ride was
long, and both baby and bear were grumpy. But
in time, they both stopped yowling and fell
asleep. I could feel both of their hearts beating
against me as I rode.

I whispered to my sister-horse, *Take me where I
need to go.*

My mare brought me to the grassy field at the
base of the mountain where there were brass
bells on every door. I waited in the field until
Melek felt me there. He seemed to know when I
needed him. I could see him look out of his door
just as if I had called to him.

When Melek arrived in the field, I was so tired
I couldn't speak. I handed him my brother,
showed him where the milk rags were for both
bear and boy, then fell asleep at his feet. I trusted
Melek with everything that was important to me,

and maybe I was a fool to do so. All the same, when I woke he was feeding my horse handfuls of tall grass. He had tied the bear cub to a small tree with a leather rope. As for Anto, he was asleep on his blanket.

Would you like to have a brother? I asked.

By now, Melek knew much of our language.

I would like to have you, he told me.

I laughed, but the laughter sounded sharp, like a rock against both of us, or an arrow, one that could indeed pierce through flesh.

I know I can't. Melek shrugged. *So instead I'll take a brother.*

The bear is his brother as well. So you'll have to take two. But let the one be a boy and the other be a bear.

Melek came close to me. He knew I was now the Queen. He saw the blue tattoos on my face, so fresh they still stung.

I will take anything you give me.

Before I left I gave him myself. Not the way they did at the festival. Not like that at all. There was no koumiss to make me dizzy, no red flower paste to put me into a trance; there was no reason to be together other than what we felt. What that was cannot be put into words. Maybe only that on that day we belonged to each other. That we had found each other in a world where it was nearly always impossible to find what had been lost. I thought of Penthe and my mother and I understood that love went beyond where we were, the snowfields and the grasslands, on into the next world and the world after that.

I made my choice. I had heard my mother the Queen say to Penthe that a Queen must always abide by her decisions. In that way she finds her strength. In a few weeks, Melek and his people would be gone. They were wanderers and might not return. They would go their way, and I would go mine. That was the way it was meant to be. After all, my dreams were of my own country. There were a thousand horses waiting for me and a thousand warriors as well. I could feel who I was in my blood. I had no need to change my name, to call myself anything other than what I was. Queen Rain.

In the morning, when I left that place, I knew

that I was made of sorrow. But sorrow is strong. It is lasting. You can't deny it or get rid of it.

I was made out of rain, but nothing could bind me.

Nothing could stop me from being who I was meant to be all along.

In the

Reign

In the reign of my Queenship my brother saved my life.

He did that when I went to get him from the priestesses. That was part of the foretelling, the part I hadn't understood: *Who you save, saves you as well.*

The decision to murder me was made by those who believed I would betray them, and who betrayed themselves instead. They came to kill me the night that I left; they assumed I would leave in the morning, as I'd said I would. They thought I was sleeping in my blankets, a hard sleep. I did not wake when Asteria and her women put their knives in me. I did not move until they rolled me over and saw my red hair, the henna tattoos on my face.

They killed my sister Io in my place.

I knew this because Penthe was waiting for me in a clearing on the far steppe, beneath a flowering tree. With her was a small and loyal group who carried my sister's body. Io was covered with honey and yellow chalk; she was wound in my blanket, sewn up with red thread from her own horse.

I thought I had no more tears, but that wasn't true.

I fell onto my knees and wept for the sister who had loved me even when I'd been cruel to her, whose heart was so open, who had always tried to protect me, and even now had taken my place.

Astella was among the group of mourners, and

my aunt Cybelle and all of her women who kept bees. Even Astella, that fierce warrior, had been crying. And not for Io. For her own cousin. The one she knew she must now defeat.

We have to go back now, Astella told me, even as I grieved. *There's no time for anything else.*

I remembered what Cybelle had once said: A Queen has no time for love.

Now I realized that a Queen had to carry her love with her, and that gave her all the time there ever would be.

If we don't remove Asteria and her women, anyone will think they have the right to go after you, Astella warned me.

In my reign would our people fight each other for the first time? Would horses ride against sister-horses? Would women who loved each other, who'd grown up together, cut each other open with scythes?

If you don't fight back, they'll think you have no courage. A Queen without courage is a worthless thing.

I turned to my aunt, the keeper of the bees. *You must do something,* Cybelle agreed. *That is your duty.*

I went to sit beside Penthe and mourn Io. I asked if I could see my sister one more time, and Penthe nodded. She wanted that, too. I took my knife and cut along the thread, then opened a small section of the blanket, so I could look into Io's face.

My sister seemed to be sleeping. I could not see the knife wounds in her back. All I could see was her face, her pale skin, the long red hair that had been braided and combed with honey. I did not understand how I could live my days in this world without Io. I didn't understand why this should happen when she wasn't even in battle, only sleeping, dreaming.

She had two hundred fathers, Penthe told me. *More even than you.*

Penthe spoke partially in our language and partially in her old language, the one she had learned when she was a slave used by any man who wanted her.

I thought I wouldn't want a daughter born from that. I thought I might drown her. Not just for my benefit, but for hers. That life was not worth living. What good is misery? Maybe I cursed her by thinking that way when she came into this world.

She wasn't cursed, I said. *Nor was I.*

So your mother told me, Penthe said. *I wish she had told you.*

Still, hearing that was a blessing to me, whether or not it was true. I sat beside Penthe as she sang Io the lullaby from the north storm country, then I tied the thread back together and closed up the blanket. I would never again see my sister's face, but now it was behind my eyes, a part of me.

What would my mother have me do? I asked Penthe. *Fight our own people?*

She would trust you to know the right thing, since you're now our Queen, as you were always meant to be.

My sister who was never born was meant to be Queen.

I was talking to a woman who had lost everything, her daughter, her beloved, her Queen, her country, even her own skin marked with two hundred tattoos that were not of her choosing.

Even a Queen can be wrong, Penthe said. *As your mother was for a very long time. You have nothing of those fifty cowards. As Io had nothing that belonged to anyone else. All of her courage was hers alone. All of your strength belongs to you.*

I went by myself to the place where my bear had been killed and asked for guidance one last time. By now the earth that had been red, then black, was yellow again. I thought that blood disappeared into the earth, just as our life disappeared from this world, but now I believed what we did and who we were was eternal. As Deborah had said.

I honored my sister the bear by chanting a prayer. Then I made my own decision. I knew what I must do. A Queen must always put her people first. I told Penthe to wait with Io for me, and I rode back with Astella and Cybelle and the others who were true to me, or true to my mother the Queen's daughter, which was the same thing.

They were waiting for us on the ridge before our city, the renegades. Everyone else was ready to fight as well, but on which side? There was confusion, the idea of sister against sister had made tempers flare. Our warriors were fully clothed for battle, with their shields and their arrows. But would they follow Asteria, or would they choose me?

Astella rode beside me. I could feel how much she wanted to reach for her bow, but she did not. We rode forward without our weapons raised.

It was a time of decision for our people. If I turned and ran, my sisters would follow and track me down. But if I faced them, what would happen then?

I stood on my horse, the way my great-grandmother was said to do whenever she spoke to her people.

Asteria has killed my sister. She's betrayed your Queen. She's no longer of our people, I said.

Come forward, Asteria shouted. *Make that be true if you can.*

She had pressed her bow to her chest, where she had sacrificed her breast for our people so that her aim would be perfect, as it was.

We will not fight against our sisters, or even those who had once been our sisters, I called back to her.

I knew what she would do before she did it.

Maybe because she had been my teacher. She shot her perfect arrow, but I had touched my mare with my knee the instant before she did and my mare leapt away. I could feel the arrow, though; it was that close, close as the wind.

And just as close, Astella's arrow in return, perfect as well, aimed to stop Asteria, not to kill her.

When Asteria fell from her horse, her women scattered, and we let them go. They raced off for the east country, not a place I'd wish on anyone, even my enemies. A place of salt and men without courage and the cold Black Sea. The warriors who fled did not hesitate long enough to help Asteria onto her great mare, which took off with the running horses, riderless.

Our people watched all this and they knew that a Queen must always put her people first. I got off my mare and walked to Asteria, my teacher, the great warrior.

You can't be our Queen, she spat. *You're nothing like your mother.* There was blood running down her arm. Our people would pull the arrow out before they sent her off, and I would make certain she was given a mare, a fast one.

If anyone wishes to go with Asteria, then go, I shouted to my people. *We will never kill our own sisters. Go in peace if you wish to.*

A few went with her. I did not look to see who or how many. I did not wish them ill or hope that the winter in the east would be any colder than ours. I had begun to think about peace and what it might feel like to a warrior.

Before I returned to where Penthe waited, I went to the smith. I asked him to put the image of one of Io's eyes on the scythe she'd returned to me, and he did so. I wanted my sister to see all that I saw each and every day I was in this world.

When he was through I asked if I could look once more into the fire.

There is nothing in this fire for a Queen, the smith said, humble before me. He was afraid of me now. I was no longer just a girl.

Then for a woman, I said.

He picked up some earth and threw it into his fire, where he magicked metal into knives and scythes. I saw so many images in the flames that I did not know which to believe.

I asked the smith if he remembered where he

came from and what his life was like before he was captured in battle.

Only in my dreams, he said.

You can go back if you want. In exchange for my scythe and for Io's. You have your freedom, I said.

The smith then gave me a gift; it was heartfelt, unasked for. A small musical thing he had made out of brass, like the one I'd seen in Melek's village; when you breathed into it, music came out.

I rode to where Penthe was waiting. There were kurgans close by, burial places for our people, but I was taking Io to the kurgan of the Queens. Penthe leaned and kissed her daughter good-bye through the wrapped felt blanket, then we lifted my sister onto my mare, and I got on behind her. I rode to the place of the Queens and as I did I wept. I would not cry again. I wept all the rest of my tears at one time, and they were well spent on my sister.

I first brought Io to the cave where Deborah was, so that Deborah's chanting could help Io find her way in the next world.

I could see that Deborah was leaving our world bit by bit. She was so old she could no longer move. There were three ravens in the cave. I saw that they were becoming her sisters and that when she left our world she would be a raven in the endless sky.

Still, Deborah used what was left of her strength to chant over Io. She did not ask what had happened, and perhaps she did not need to. She had the augury after all. Greeya made us the ritual funeral dinner, some of the horsemeat I had brought with me.

What happened to the Black Horse? Deborah asked me.

He ran across the fields to people who would take care of him.

Deborah smiled and motioned me closer when Greeya went to gather wood for the fire.

You won't see me again.

I could tell this was true from the sound of the priestess's voice. It was barely a whisper, as though she were already leaving.

If you want anything, ask now.

Perhaps we were not meant to know what our

fortunes would bring, but I asked for the augury one last time. When Deborah agreed I went to get the box of bones and shells and stones. The truth was inside that box, if you knew enough to understand it.

I helped Deborah to sit up and she threw the augury. It fell like rain at our feet.

Everything will change. All we can do is pray for a day when there are no warriors and no wars for them to fight.

That was all the priestess could tell me, but it was enough.

To protect me from evil, Deborah made a spell of my own blood, which she took from a gash in my arm and mixed with some of her herbs. She painted my face with it. Two stripes of red beneath each eye, mixing with the blue of our people. Then she gave me something she had been saving under her blanket. My mother's pearl ring. The pearl had come from far, far away, in the time of our great-grandmothers.

She told me to give it to the next Queen. She hoped it would be you.

I thanked the priestess and bowed before her. I felt the truth in everything she'd said.

At the mouth of the cave I told Greeya that when the time came, I would return and help her honor Deborah with a funeral. But Greeya said no; it was best for her to do that alone. I understood. I had come here alone with Io, and I went alone with her to the catacombs of the Queens.

It was late when I got there, so I rode inside and tied my horse up. She stayed steady as I lifted Io, who was now so heavy she might have been turning already to stone. I took her to a small chamber in the house of the Queens. It should have been my chamber, but my sister took my place.

All that night, I sang the lullaby from the north storm country to Io. I didn't want to leave her in this cold dark place. Because she had no weapons I left the musical instrument the smith had made so that she would enter the next world with the lullaby still with her.

When I left I knew I would not return to the catacombs of the Queens until my own time came. Our world would be different now; everything was changing. I thought of the well we would build in our city, to ensure we always had fresh water, and the tents we would make, year-round structures with wooden doors and brass bells. To journey back and forth meant to fight constantly; if we stayed in one place our country might be smaller, but it would be easier to protect, especially now that Asteria and her women were claiming the east. The time we had used for traveling we would use for other concerns. We could think of things other than war. We might even think of peace.

I thought of our breath and our blood, how eventually it would fall on the yellow earth and disappear. I thought of how my mother's pearl ring fit me perfectly, as though it had been made for me. In the end, our people would decide for themselves. Some would follow Asteria, some would follow me. Maybe that's the way it was supposed to be. Each woman makes her own fortune, her own decisions.

I stopped as I always did at the place of the bear, but I didn't stay long. I had no time to think of

Melek, or my brother, or even my sister, Io. My people could not wait for me. My country could not wait.

As for me, I was ready to return as the Queen. I had made something out of my sorrow. I had stitched it together with a rope made of hair from the tail of my mare; I had used the bones of my grandmothers and my mother and my sister as needles. I chanted my gratitude all the way home. Thank you to my sister the bear, to my sister-horse, to the goddess above us, thank you for letting me be who I am, for letting me ride into whatever fortune we made together. Thank you for letting me be Rain and no one else.

It was the ending of something. It was the beginning of something.

I rode harder.

I rode faster.

It was my country, my time, my age, my beginning. I went across the yellow earth, over the black rocks, through the streams where the water was so cold you could never forget winter, into a place where the sky reached on forever.

References to Amazon women have appeared in literature and art throughout time, most notably in ancient Greece. The remains of warrior women have also been found in graves around the Black Sea; their cultures may be the factual basis for the Amazon myths of the heroic age. In a time when nomads ruled the steppes of Russia and the Ukraine, there appears to have been women who knew war as well as any man. Let us hope they also knew peace.

Deepest gratitude to my editor, Andrea Spooner,
for support, kindness, and wisdom.

Thank you to Alyssa Morris and Matt Mahurin
for their visions.

Thanks also to Sangeeta Mehta
and to Elizabeth Eulberg.

To my grandmothers, thank you for every word.
I listened.